Exiled

The Rykfallinn Chronicles, Volume 1

Kristina Hall

Published by Kristina Hall, 2023.

This is a work of fiction. Similarities to real people, places, or events are entirely coincidental.

EXILED

First edition. August 3, 2023.

Copyright © 2023 Kristina Hall.

ISBN: 979-8223354154

Written by Kristina Hall.

Also by Kristina Hall

A Better Country
Strangers and Pilgrims
To the Uttermost

Kentucky Midnight
Midnight Will Come
Darkness Draws Near
Shadows Close In

Refuge
Fled for Refuge
Refuge from the Storm
Place of Refuge

Science Falsely So Called
Things Not Seen

Stand

The Dry Springs Chronicles
Trouble in Dry Springs

The Moretti Trilogy
Promises Unbroken
Mercy Undeserved
Truth Unshaken

The Rykfallinn Chronicles
Exiled

Praise for Exiled

The first installment in a series, *Exiled* is a thoughtful story with a unique western twist. Featuring themes of redemption and selflessness in a lawless wilderness, Hall's characters grapple with the need to survive despite injustice. It will keep you reading and leave you wanting more!

—Michaela Bush, author of *A Dance of Rebels*

Complete with Kristina Hall's trademark suspense, *Exiled* skillfully merges the rugged flavor of the Wild West with the intriguing novelty of a fantasy world. When you reach the end, you'll be craving more of this heart-pounding adventure with its endearing characters, precarious shootouts, and perilous secrets!

—Saraina Whitney, author of *To Be Loved* in the *Tell Me You Love Me* anthology

Western vibes meet a fantasy setting in this suspenseful tale! Hall has crafted a unique story world full of danger, secrets, and shadowed pasts. Hold on to your hats—it's about to get western.

—M.L. Milligan, author of *Undefined* in the *Seize the Fight* anthology

Hall combines an engaging plot and a subgenre not often used to create a story rich in worldbuilding and faith. Readers of Christian fantasy will not want to miss this captivating tale of danger and gentle romance.

—Madisyn Carlin, author of The Redwyn Chronicles

An epic adventure where fantasy and western collide in a world of dragons, gamblers, and wastelands. Where the smallest infraction leads to exile and danger lurks around every corner. Absolutely delightful read!

—Kaytlin Phillips, author of *World of Silence* and coauthor of The Dragon Prince Chronicles

Kristina Hall's *Exiled* takes the idea of a western to another level with a gripping plot and charming characters set amidst a familiar yet fantastical land. Sure to be a favorite among readers who enjoy Christian westerns and fantasy!

—Vanessa Hall, author of the Grace Sufficient series

Chapter 1

At half past midnight, the knock finally came.

I dropped my book, swept from the bedroom, and rushed down the hall. My husband of just two weeks was home after a week-long mission.

My footsteps echoed around me as I hurried down the steps. Breath coming much too hard, I stilled before the front door and fished my key from my skirt pocket.

The lantern sitting on the small table by the door filled the entryway with warm light.

With a twist, I unlocked the door and threw it open.

Agnarr stared at me, mouth set in a grim line and broad shoulders drooping. The rain that'd been tapping on the roof ever since sunset plastered his brown hair against his head.

And four hulking men—all clad in the brown uniform of the king's army—stood behind him.

Something hard and foreboding darkened Agnarr's features, but I pressed a smile to my lips. "You've brought guests." Even after a week away from me, he must not care much about my company.

One of the men lurking behind him—a tall fellow with a bushy black beard—barked a laugh.

Agnarr was the captain of the royal guard. Not someone who would be on the army's bad side.

Yet something was going on here. Something completely wrong.

"Agnarr?"

He hung his head.

The black-bearded soldier shoved Agnarr to the side, and chains clanked. "By order of the king, you, Svana Vev, and your husband, Agnarr Vev, are to be exiled to the Rykfallinn Wastelands."

I'd fallen asleep while reading. I was having a nightmare. None of this could be real.

Agnarr—honorable, diligent, law-abiding Agnarr—would never be among those exiled.

"Your orders have to be wrong." And my voice had no call to be so tremulous.

A gust of wind blew through the door, and drops of cold rain spit in my face.

The soldier tipped back his head and laughed. "I assure you they're not, my lady. Now extend your hands, and let's do this the easy way. There's no use in running. I've got men stationed at the back door and around the sides of the house."

Agnarr stood motionless, hands behind his back, head still down.

I held out my hands—my shaking hands.

The soldier drew irons from his belt and clamped them around my wrists. Then he attached a chain to the irons and tugged me forward. "Let's get moving."

His fellow soldiers forced Agnarr into motion.

Rain spattered my head and shoulders, and the wind whipped my dress around my legs.

The two-story houses on either side of the street stood dark and still, but the tread of the soldiers' boots against the cobblestones thundered above the patter of the rain.

"Under what charges are we being exiled?"

Was it something I'd done? Had my past caught up to me here after so many years? But if that were the case, they wouldn't have exiled Agnarr with me. Only heads of households had the privilege—if one could call it that—of having their families exiled along with them.

The black-bearded soldier glanced over his shoulder. "He put the king's son in danger."

A lie. Agnarr would never knowingly put any of the people he'd been tasked to protect in danger. "That must be wrong."

The soldier shrugged. "The king has given his orders. Both of you are to be exiled."

The words hit me with the force of a dozen blows.

Exiled just like Mama and Papa had been four months before I'd been born. Yet this time, I wouldn't be allowed to leave the wastelands when I reached a certain age. This time, I would be an exile myself.

My sodden hem wrapped around my ankles, and I stumbled.

The irons jerked at my wrists, and I regained my balance, teeth clenched against the breath that wanted to hiss out.

"Hurry up. We've got to make the train on time. Then it's a hundred-mile trip to the wall."

A hundred miles until we reached the wall that separated Fairrlande from the lawless Rykfallinn Wastelands. Then we would have to cross fifteen miles of desolate desert to reach Long Gulch, the closest settlement.

Yet before that, we'd be tattooed as exiles.

A shiver coursed up my spine. How many times had I brushed my fingers across the thick lines on Mama's and Papa's left shoulders as a child?

"The charges must be wrong." If only I had some sort of authority behind those words.

"Svana." Agnarr's voice was nothing but a rasp.

But behind that one word were a thousand, all of them proclaiming that there wasn't a single thing I could do to change what was happening.

I forced one foot in front of the other.

The rain picked up, slithering down the sides of my face and soaking my dress.

I should enjoy it. Once we traversed the tunnel leading through the Fairrlande Mountains, I'd be wishing for moisture.

Exiled.

Agnarr planted one foot in front of the other, the parched ground unyielding beneath his boots.

Exiled because the king's son had slipped away from his handler and headed straight for the tavern.

Yes, as captain of the royal guard, he had to take responsibility for his men and their actions. But exile? Exile that condemned him and Svana to the wastelands? Exile that inked an *X* on his wife's shoulder? Exile that dragged her from the safety of their home and stranded her in this desert?

She walked beside him, each step measured and sure. Yet her head drooped, and that *X* blazed a dark path across her shoulder.

He never should've married her. He should've ignored the king's law that declared everyone who turned thirty had to marry. He never should've attended that ball, never should've asked her to dance.

Yet he had, and now she suffered the consequences of those decisions.

"I'm sorry." The first words she'd spoken since they stepped off that train.

"No." He was the one who should be apologizing. Not her.

She tucked a copper tangle behind her ear, then turned those hazel eyes on him.

She saw too much. All too much.

He turned his face away from her.

"I know how much being the captain of the guard meant to you."

It meant less than nothing when this was what it earned him.

He should've been a blacksmith, a banker, a farmer. Anything that wouldn't have ended with exile.

Wind heavy with grit blasted his face.

The barren, rocky landscape stretched out ahead, cloaked by the gray light of early morning.

They'd come a mile from the wall at most.

"Fourteen more until we reach Long Gulch."

Uncanny how she could read him like that. Especially given she'd known him only a month and he'd been away a majority of that time.

Not a good start to their marriage. Then again, neither was exile.

"When the sun gets too hot, we'll find shelter and wait it out." Then keep traveling.

They'd likely reach Long Gulch sometime during the night.

Long Gulch and all the dangers it held.

But he had to find work—and a place for Svana to stay.

She cleared her throat. "There should be a spring about halfway between here and Long Gulch."

At least she had some knowledge of this land—enough that she'd made the trip to the wall five years ago and gained entrance to Fairrlande.

"What do you know about Long Gulch?"

She glanced down, hair falling to veil her face. "There's not much to it except for gambling halls, brothels, and saloons. It's the worst of the towns in the wastelands."

"The next closest town?"

"Dead Ridge." She let out a rough breath. "Despite its name, it's one of the more peaceful towns out here."

She would know. She'd spent twenty-five years of her life in the wastelands.

She stared at him, expression haunted. "I'm bound to meet someone who recognizes me."

Given that she'd been a renowned gambler, that was no surprise. "No one's going to bother you."

He might not be a gunfighter, but he knew how to use his fists and feet.

The only weapons the king had left him with.

Svana looked down at her shoulder and winced.

The breath she'd hissed as they'd tattooed her had hurt a hundred times worse than the needle against his own skin.

Those men had better pray they never got exiled and met him on some dark street.

"It's fine." Softness touched her features. "You can't turn back time."

If he could, he'd chain the king's brat of a son hand and foot and set a watch of four guards over him. If he could, he'd break the chains the soldiers had clamped on his wrists and whisk Svana off somewhere they'd never find her.

But wishing for what could never be was a waste of time.

He forced a breath into his lungs to keep from shouting words that didn't belong on the tongue of a child of God. "Tell me if you need to stop."

She lifted her chin. "I'll be ready to stop when the sun gets too high."

Stubborn as the day was long. Yet that iron will would benefit her in a land like this.

She again glanced at the *X* on her shoulder. "You're okay?"

"Yes." The ink on his shoulder was the least of his worries.

A raucous combination of music cut through the night that surrounded Long Gulch. Jazz. A jig. A jaunty piano tune.

Distant shouts, laughter, and the occasional shot punctuated it all.

Nothing had changed.

Weight pressed over my shoulders, and I lowered myself onto a boulder.

Long Gulch stretched ahead and below, filled with lights and at least a hundred shadowy figures moving through the streets.

A cold night wind whipped around me, and Agnarr's big hand settled on my right shoulder. "We're safer here than down there."

Yes. Better to enter Long Gulch when the troublemakers were still in bed nursing their hangovers or working.

He squeezed my shoulder. "Get some sleep. It'll be morning soon enough."

Why ever had he asked to marry me? A man like him could've had his pick of women.

Yet for some reason, he'd chosen me.

Much more than likely just to fill the law's requirement.

The same reason I'd gone to the ball that night. But I'd gotten the far better end of the deal.

A man strong of faith and character. A man who treated me gently and with honor.

Yet sooner or later, he would figure out that I was no prize.

I pushed to my feet, every muscle and bone aching, and brushed a kiss to his whiskery cheek. "Good night."

He drew me into an embrace that avoided my tender left shoulder. "I'd build a fire, but it'd draw too much attention."

I rested my cheek against his shoulder. The scent of sweat, dust, and the faintest hint of soap surrounded me. "It's not that cold."

And even if it were, I'd rather shiver than fight off bandits.

He stepped back and took his warmth with him.

I settled on a patch of dry ground that was currently free of scorpions and rattlers. Millions of stars hung overhead, studding the black sky, and the moon bathed the land in its blue light.

Agnarr strode to the boulder I'd occupied earlier and sat, shoulders rigid.

He wouldn't sleep. No, he'd watch. He'd watch himself straight into exhaustion.

Heaviness tugged at my eyelids, and the cacophony of music swirled around me.

The smoke in the air. The fire of whiskey on my tongue. The cards in my hand. The table full of men sitting around me. The satin of my dress brushing against my arms. The clink of gold as I raked my winnings toward me.

Yet that life was no longer mine.

I eased into a sitting position.

The shadow that was Agnarr shifted. "Can't sleep?"

Heaviness clung to me as I stood and crossed to where he sat. "I was ... thinking."

"You want to go back to it?"

He didn't trust me. "No."

Silence stretched between us. Weighty silence.

Yes, I could easily slip back into that life. My skills hadn't left me—no, they were too ingrained for that. I would never forget how to cheat carefully enough that I didn't find myself full of lead. I'd never forget how to slip money from men's pockets when they weren't paying attention.

But I was no longer that woman. Through Jesus, I would resist the draw of the wealth, power, and thrill of that former life.

I climbed onto the boulder, and the coolness of the rock seeped through my skirt. Strange tightness claimed my throat. "You don't believe me?"

Not that I even had to ask. His silence had said it all.

And why should he trust me? I was scarcely more than a stranger to him.

"I believe you."

Did he only say that because he thought it was what I wanted to hear?

Yet he'd done nothing to prove himself untrustworthy.

"Thank you."

That silence again settled in.

The wind swept my hair into my face, and chills crawled across my skin. Too bad my left sleeve had been ripped away. It would've provided a bit more warmth.

He wrapped his arm around me, again avoiding my left shoulder, and I leaned into his solid warmth.

If I had to be exiled, at least I had him beside me.

"I'll find work tomorrow. I know you're hungry."

I could last weeks without food, but a shakiness had settled in my limbs. "Shall I work too?"

The sooner we could earn money, the faster we could leave Long Gulch and find a permanent place to settle.

He turned his head toward me. "As long as it's a safe, decent job."

"From what I can remember, there's a café, a hotel, even a laundry."

All jobs I would've turned up my nose at years ago.

He nodded. "I don't plan for us to stay here long. Just long enough to get some supplies and a couple of horses. I don't want to settle in the worst town in the wastelands."

I drew a slow breath. "What I said earlier ... about people recognizing me. I didn't mean to imply that they'd wish to harm me. I was well liked."

"You shouldn't be here." His voice came low.

"Please don't blame yourself."

He jerked to his feet, taking his warmth with him. "I should've stopped that stupid kid from sneaking away."

Arguing with him wouldn't help anything. But ... "You were the best man the king had. He shouldn't punish you so harshly for his own son's misbehavior."

He turned his back to me, his shoulders as unyielding as iron. "What's done is done."

The truth that no debate could change.

My shoulder bore the tattoo, and I'd never again be allowed beyond that wall.

We had to build a life in the Rykfallinn Wastelands—if such a thing were possible in a land that valued violence above all else.

Dawn etched the horizon as he descended from the rocky slope where he and Svana had spent the night.

He jumped down from a jagged boulder, then turned and offered his hand to Svana.

She took it and landed beside him. Dust streaked her sunburned face, and skin peeled from her cracking lips.

The sooner he could earn enough to get them supplied and away from this lawless town, the better.

He released her hand and set off. "I'll find work, then we'll see about getting you a position."

She nodded. "I know the couple who owns the hotel. At least I did back then."

In five years, the place could've changed hands multiple times.

"They were kind to me when I stayed there when I was visiting Long Gulch, and they always told me the truth."

Bits of crushed rock ground beneath the leather soles of his boots. "It'd be good if we could work at the same place."

Then he could keep an eye on things and make sure no one bothered her.

She pulled her hair around to her right side. "The Barrons—the couple who owns the hotel—always used to keep a guard or two on staff to make sure no one got out of control."

He could go from being captain of the royal guard to keeping riffraff under control.

Now that was a promotion.

But as long as it earned him the needed funds, he'd take it. "That'd work."

Yet Svana's acquaintances might not even own the hotel anymore.

Long Gulch stretched ahead, shadows hanging around the buildings. A few figures moseyed down the main street.

At least it was a whole lot calmer than it'd been last night.

Yet danger could lurk even in places that seemed calm and innocent. One too many incidents had taught him that much.

The crack of gunfire through a still forest. The charge of a man from a dark alley.

Calm or no calm, he couldn't let his guard down.

Svana slowed, her breaths coming a little too hard.

The sleepless night on the train, the fifteen-mile walk through the desert with little water and no food, and another near sleepless night had to have taken a toll on her whether she'd admit it or not.

If her acquaintances still owned the hotel, maybe they could be persuaded to let her eat and rest some before she started working.

He could start working right away to prove they hadn't come to take advantage of the Barrons's generosity.

"Do you need to rest?"

She lifted her hand to cover a yawn. "I know I'm poking."

She'd taken what he'd said as an insult?

A hint of a smile curved up her dry lips. "I'm all right. Just worn out."

Worn out because that brat of a kid couldn't control his need for drink. Worn out because he hadn't stopped that kid. Worn out because the king had refused to give him the thirty lashes he'd ordered doled out to the guards on watch and had instead chosen to exile him.

"It's not much farther." An edge of something—hesitation or maybe apprehension—colored her voice.

No, Long Gulch lay just ahead. A hundred paces would have them to the structures on the outskirts.

I ask Your protection, Lord. Allow my reflexes to be quick and my eyes to be sharp. And thank You for Your presence.

Not even the wastelands could keep Him away.

Step by step erased the hundred paces.

The buildings crawled by—a ramshackle conglomeration of homes, saloons, brothels, gambling halls, and businesses.

The café stood darkened—both of its front windows shattered and its sign hanging by one chain.

Too bad.

If it'd been open—and in business—he'd have washed dishes or done some other such labor in exchange for a couple of meals.

"I suppose the café isn't an option for work." Svana cleared her throat. "I hope Mrs. Cunningworth is all right." She glanced right and left. "The hotel's up ahead. It's on the right side of First Street."

Hopefully, it hadn't suffered the same fate as the café.

He hung a right onto what had to be First Street. Sure enough, the hotel—a two-story plank structure—stood tall and proud to his right.

And lantern light glowed from the downstairs windows.

"Their name is still on the sign." Svana let out a breath heavy with relief.

He stepped in close to her. "Don't mention my work." Nothing good could come of anyone out here discovering he'd been captain of the royal guard.

She gave a quick nod and paled.

He tugged open the hotel door for her, then followed her inside.

Worn red carpet covered the floor, and a brass chandelier hung over the front desk.

The thin, gray-haired woman behind the desk glanced up with a smile. "Morning. May I help you?"

Either this wasn't one of Svana's acquaintances or the woman had a poor memory.

Svana crossed to the desk. "Mrs. Barron, it's Svana."

The woman—Mrs. Barron—beamed, rounded the desk, and took Svana in her arms. "Svana! I didn't recognize you without your cosmetics. It's so good to see you."

He slid his hands in his pockets and leaned against the wall.

Mrs. Barron rested her hands on Svana's shoulders and eased her back. Svana flinched.

Mrs. Barron jerked her hands away, eyes going wide. "Oh, your poor shoulder and face. I'll tell Doc to put some salve on that sunburn."

The woman didn't question why Svana's shoulder bore the tattoo? Then again, she was likely an exile herself and the majority of her customers were exiles.

Svana glanced over her shoulder and shot a shaky smile his way. "This is my husband, Agnarr Vev."

He stepped forward and nodded in the woman's direction. "Agnarr, this is Mrs. Barron."

He forced his lips into a smile that cracked and stung. "It's good to meet you." Best to get to the point. "Do you have any open positions around here?"

"We're short a couple of maids and a guard." She studied him, then laughed." But I don't expect you'd be interested in being a maid."

He chuckled. "We're just looking for short-term jobs, but I'd be obliged if you'd consider me as a guard. And Svana would be interested in a maid position."

"Of course." Mrs. Barron smiled at Svana. "I'd hire Svana and any relation of hers in a heartbeat. But I'll have to talk things over with Doc, and I expect he'll want to interview you."

As he should.

"Come along." Mrs. Barron stepped toward a doorway and motioned for them to follow. "You both need to get cleaned up and get some food in your systems. I'm sorry to say it, but you look like death warmed over."

An apt description.

He followed Svana and Mrs. Barron up a flight of stairs.

Mrs. Barron stopped outside a door and glanced over her shoulder. "If you'll both wait out here, I'll speak to Doc."

He nodded in acknowledgment.

Mrs. Barron disappeared inside and closed the door behind her.

"It's their living quarters." Svana faced him and combed her fingers through her hair.

Similar doors lined the hallway, likely leading to rooms for rent.

She lowered her hands to her sides. "I'm glad they're here."

At first glance, Mrs. Barron seemed trustworthy. Whether she truly was remained to be seen.

The door swept open, and Mrs. Barron poked her head into the hallway. "Come right in. I'll get some food for you while you talk to Doc."

He stepped through the doorway after Svana and shut the door behind him.

Mrs. Barron led them through a sitting room of sorts and into a dining room. "Have a seat. I'll have something for you to eat in a few minutes."

Svana's stomach rumbled, and she pressed her hand to it.

Mrs. Barron laughed and bustled from the room. "I'll hurry."

He pulled out a chair for Svana, then sat beside her.

A short man with gray hair and a sharp gaze strode into the room.

Agnarr pushed to his feet and extended his hand. "Agnarr Vev."

The man shook his hand, his grip firm. "A pleasure to meet you. I'm Doc Barron. My wife said you're looking for work."

He nodded.

Svana stepped to his side. "Doc."

Barron grinned and took Svana's hand in both of his. "It's good to see you." He nodded to the table. "Both of you sit down so we can talk about work."

Chapter 2

"What happened, dear?" The lines around Mrs. Barron's eyes deepened.

I set my fork on my empty plate.

Doc and Agnarr stood on the other side of the room, deep in conversation.

I licked my dehydrated lips. "I can't give you many details, but Agnarr was exiled—not for anything of a criminal nature—and I was exiled along with him."

Mrs. Barron nodded. "I'm sorry. I remember how thrilled you were when your twenty-fifth birthday rolled around and you were able to leave for Fairrlande."

It'd been a good five years spent mostly with Grandma and Grandpa and the rest of my extended family—family I'd never see again on earth unless they were exiled as well.

Something hard and tight expanded through my chest. Had they found out I'd been exiled yet?

Please comfort them, Lord. Please don't let them grieve me.

They'd already been through this once with Mama and Papa. They shouldn't have to face it again with me.

Yet maybe it'd help them to know I was with Agnarr.

"I'm sorry." Mrs. Barron reached across the table and rested her hand on mine. "I know it's hard."

I pressed a smile to my face. "He's still with me."

A truth I had to cling to.

Mrs. Barron's face softened. "He is. You don't know how glad I am that He is."

And she and Doc had been His faithful witnesses whenever they saw me.

"When did you marry? Your husband seems like a fine man."

He was. Much finer than I deserved. "We got married a little over two weeks ago."

There was so much I could ask her, so much about loving and caring for a husband that was so far out of my league.

"How long have you known each other?"

"Around a month." My face heated.

Mrs. Barron gave a low laugh. "You always did procrastinate."

Yes, but I'd gone to many social events in Fairrlande hoping to meet a future husband in the years I'd lived there. Yet the fact that I'd been born and raised in the wastelands had turned away all the prospects—all except for a certain desperate captain of the royal guard.

"He's a believer. He's hardworking. He treats me kindly."

No, we had nothing like the love Doc and Mrs. Barron shared, but they'd also been married for a good forty years.

Mrs. Barron smiled. "He seems like a good man. You two look wonderful together."

Mrs. Barron must have an inflated view of my looks. Agnarr was much more handsome than I was beautiful.

Yes, I could measure up to the wastelands' standard of beauty if I donned a low-cut dress and used enough cosmetics, yet in Fairrlande, I'd been nothing special.

"Not as good as you and Doc." I grinned at her.

She blushed. "You really think so?"

"I think you're a striking couple." And their kindness made them all the more so.

She waved a hand in front of her face. "And now you've resorted to flattery. You know you could just ask me for another piece of cake."

Mrs. Barron knew I'd never been given to flattery. "It was a delicious piece of cake." And it'd been made finer still by the meals I'd missed since the exile.

She tapped both hands to the table's polished surface. "That settles it. I shall cut you another piece."

Doc turned from his conversation with Agnarr. "Let everything settle for an hour or two. You don't want to be sick."

Wise words. Even if every starved inch of my body screamed for at least another piece or two of that cake. Even if some would say it was far too early for any amount of cake.

Mrs. Barron laughed. "You'll just have to be patient, my dear."

It appeared my poker face had taken leave of me.

"I'll show you to your room." Mrs. Barron stood. "I know you'll want to bathe and rest."

Agnarr stiffened. "I'm ready to start working."

Doc gave him a nod. "There will be time enough for that tomorrow."

Agnarr's shoulders didn't ease in the slightest. "I'm not here to impose."

I should say something. Yet heaviness meandered through my muscles, and my eyelids drooped.

"You're not imposing." Doc's voice came as calm as ever. "We don't treat our friends—or our employees—poorly."

No, they'd always been kind. Far, far more kind than I deserved.

Unbidden tears pricked my eyes, and I blinked them back.

Mrs. Barron offered a gentle smile. "You've got to be exhausted. I can't even imagine."

Yet she must be able to. She and Doc had made the same journey after Doc had been unable to save the wife of a man with far too many connections.

Agnarr let out a breath laced with weariness. "We'll rest today and work tomorrow."

"Good." Doc gave him a friendly slap on his right shoulder. "Wouldn't do at all for me to fire a man for insubordination before he'd even worked a minute."

Mrs. Barron chuckled. "Insubordination indeed. This hotel is most definitely not part of the military."

Doc grinned. "The term can be used outside of the military."

Mrs. Barron's chuckle turned to a full-fledged laugh. "Come along. I shall show you all to your room."

I struggled to my aching feet and trudged after her, Agnarr's footsteps a steady thud behind me.

"Here you are." She paused in front of a door identical to the others lining the hallway. Well, it was identical to them save for the room number. "If there's anything you need, just let me know."

She handed me a key, then drew me into a tight hug.

Oh, the prickle of tears gained new life.

I swallowed them back and eased away.

I had lost much, but I'd also regained much.

A roof over his head, food in his stomach, and a new set of clothes on his back.

But he hadn't worked for any of it.

He poured a glass of water, then dropped into the straight-backed chair to the right of the dresser.

Svana slept, blankets cast aside due to the heat and nightgown tangled around her knees.

Shouts, laughter, and music that hadn't let up for at least a few hours crashed through the curtained window.

The sooner he had enough money for weapons, supplies, and transportation the better.

Svana stirred and eased onto one elbow, blinking through the daze of sleep. "How long have you been awake?"

He shrugged. Odd hours and little sleep were nothing new.

She swung her feet over the side of the bed and yawned. "It's not as late as I thought. I feel like I slept for days."

Evening dimmed the room, yet night hadn't fully arrived.

But when it did, the cacophony below would likely take on new life.

"Just a few hours." He pushed to his feet and passed her the glass of water.

She guzzled it like she still stood in that desert. "Thank you." She frowned at the window. "It's louder than I remembered."

Being away for five years would do it.

He strode from one side of the room to the other, the stiff muscles in his legs loosening.

"Are you hungry?"

He gestured to the tray Mrs. Barron had brought by while Svana had still been sleeping. "I already ate."

More charity.

He'd be working at least several extra days to pay the Barrons back for the clothes and all the food.

She wandered to the dresser and selected a slice of bread and a few pieces of cheese.

A shot cracked from below, followed by a bunch of yelling.

Lawless idiots.

The last thing he needed was a stray slug tearing through the hotel's plank walls and hitting Svana or him.

"What do they do for work?"

She lowered herself to the side of the bed and crossed her ankles. "Most around here work in the mines."

Guarding the hotel was a far sight easier than that kind of backbreaking labor.

Another shot split the evening.

"It must pay pretty well if they've got money to be wasting ammo and yipping it up every night."

She finished off the bread and cheese. "I'd never step foot in one of the mines. I don't care how much they paid me."

"You're afraid of the dark?" She was his wife, yet he knew so little about her.

She raised both eyebrows. "I'm more afraid of however many tons of rock crashing down on me."

Not a pleasant way to go, but there were worse.

"And ..." She gave a light laugh. "I don't like being dirty."

"That's why you took twice as long as me to take a bath." He leaned against the wall opposite of where she sat.

She flopped her braid over her shoulder. "And I have this. It takes a little more time to wash than your hair."

"Excuses."

She leaned one shoulder against the headboard. "I'm sorry I'm not as good of a wife as Mrs. Barron is."

Where had that come from? "That's crazy talk."

She pressed her lips together.

"I married you. Not Mrs. Barron."

If anything, she should be regretting marrying him. She could've married a fellow who hadn't gotten himself exiled.

She rubbed her forehead. "I suppose I shouldn't have said that. My brain's not fully awake yet."

He'd never been one for emotional declarations, but ... "I love you."

She blinked at him like he'd spoken a foreign language.

No, he didn't love her as well as he should. He didn't even come close to loving her as Christ loved His church.

He pushed away from the wall and sat beside her.

A gentle smile curved her lips. "I love you too."

He leaned in and kissed her. Maybe that would show his love better than a few words.

Her hands rose to the back of his neck and drew him closer.

A shot thundered, and he pulled away.

Lawless place.

Faint lines etched around her eyes and across her forehead.

Seemed he wouldn't be getting much sleep tonight. No, his ears were too attuned to the slightest abnormal noise.

Because in those noises lay the first warnings of trouble.

She sighed. "I thought I'd be used to it, but I'm not."

And she shouldn't be. "We'll be out of here as soon as possible."

She nodded a few too many times. "I'm just glad the Barrons are still here."

Yes, they did have much to be thankful for.

"It's good to see them again."

"Were you in Long Gulch a lot?"

She stared at the wall. "I drifted around. But whenever I came through here, I'd stay at the hotel."

"You traveled alone?" Sure, she'd spoken of being respected, but that didn't stop criminals bent on harm.

She toyed with the end of her braid, the repetitive movement more distant than nervous. "No. I paid several men who were good with their guns to see to it that no trouble came near me."

Several men who'd likely worshiped the ground she'd walked on.

She touched his arm. "They were employees. Nothing more."

She shouldn't be able to read him so well so much of the time. "You're going to scare somebody doing that."

Her lips twitched. "Oh? Are you saying I scare you?"

She went from solemn to flirty in a matter of seconds.

All the better. She didn't need to see his jealousy for any longer than she already had.

"No." He spoke the word with a grin. "Nothing scares me."

She laughed. "You're a bad liar."

"I'd rather not be skilled at deception."

Her laughter faded. "What scares you? I had to confess that I don't like mines."

No way was he answering that. "Let me have a little pride." There was enough terror in what lay before them without him confessing to it.

"All right." She shot him a grin. "Hang on to that pride of yours." She cocked her head in the slightest. "Even if that sounds like really bad advice."

He stood. "I have no fears, and you always give perfect advice."

She snorted. "And we live in a very confused land."

No. Worse than that.

A confused land where danger lurked behind every rock, cactus, and plank building.

Did people realize how much dirt and debris came into the hotel on their boots and shoes?

I swept a few pieces of straw and a cigarette butt into the growing pile in the hotel's second-floor hallway.

Mrs. Barron poked her head into the hallway. "I've got the fresh linens ready whenever you're finished sweeping."

"Thank you." I smiled at her. "I'm just about finished."

"Take your time. I don't want you overworking yourself after everything you've been through."

I coaxed the pile of debris into my dustpan. "I'm feeling well."

And there wasn't a single reason to slouch on my first day of work. I needed to earn the money they were paying me.

She studied me the way Grandma always had when she was trying to figure out if I were being completely honest with her or pushing myself beyond what was healthy.

Unwelcome tightness clutched my throat, and I dashed a stray piece of straw into the dustpan.

I couldn't allow homesickness to mess up my first day of work. Not when the Barrons had been kind enough to give me this position in the first place.

"Svana?"

I swallowed past the tightness. If I looked up at her, she'd see the emotions I was restraining and I wouldn't be able to restrain them anymore. "I'll be down for the linens in just a few minutes."

"I know." Too much softness lingered in her tone.

I needed my poker face.

Yet the creaking stairs signaled her departure.

I gave the hallway a quick sweep to capture the bits of dirt I'd missed.

The stairs again squeaked, and a well-dressed fellow strutted down the hall. He tipped his head at me. "I promise I haven't brought any dirt in with me."

"Thank you. I appreciate that."

He stilled and cocked his head. "Do I know you?"

I held back a sigh. It was bound to happen sooner or later. "I don't believe you look familiar to me."

No, with his brown hair, brown eyes, and average build, he fit the description of hundreds of men I'd seen.

He studied me, then snapped his fingers. "I know you. You're that lady gambler who beat me out of a bunch of money six or seven years ago."

This time, I did sigh. "I …"

He laughed. "What're you doing here sweeping the hall when you could be down at one of the saloons raking it in?" He gestured to the steps. "Come on. I've got money rattling around in my pocket. Let's head on down there."

"I'm working here now."

Would it sound boastful and self-righteous to declare that I was a Christian now, that I no longer wanted to earn my living through cheating, deception, and thievery? If I didn't declare such a thing, would I seem like I was ashamed of my Savior?

He waved a hand through the air, turned his back on me, and stepped into his room.

So much for witnessing to him.

Weight settled over my shoulders. *Please help me do better next time.*

I headed downstairs via the narrow staircase reserved for employees, returned the broom and dustpan to the supply closet, and collected the basket of clean linens.

Agnarr stood in a doorway leading to the lobby, his back to me, the revolver belted to his hip and the confident set of his shoulders a good deterrent to anyone who might think to cause trouble.

I wouldn't bother him when he was working.

He glanced over his shoulder. "Everything going okay?"

So much for not bothering him. His hearing was a little too sharp.

I dipped a nod and propped the basket on my hip. "I'm off to make some beds."

"Watch out for the bedbugs." He quirked a smile.

At least I'd married a man with a sense of humor. Even if he used that sense of humor to remind me of things that were better not considered.

I shot him a mock grimace, then climbed the back staircase.

Bedbugs indeed.

The little nasties had better not make their presence known while I changed the linens—or anytime after.

Doc Barron exited his and Mrs. Barron's suite. "Morning, Svana."

"Good morning." Not that he'd just gotten up. Mrs. Barron had said he'd been out since well before dawn ordering and picking up supplies.

He folded his arms across his chest. "I hear a guest recognized you. Do I need to take care of anything?"

The fellow must've said something to him. "Was there a complaint?"

"No. He was only wondering where you'd been all these years and how we'd convinced you to work here."

"Oh." As long as he hadn't complained about how I did my new job. "He didn't bother me. Thank you for asking."

He stroked his well-trimmed beard with a couple of fingers. "If someone does bother you, you tell me. I don't stand for that kind of treatment toward my employees."

"Of course." Not that I would go running to him for anything but major offenses. I was well versed in dealing with small slights, and I wasn't here to cause him or Mrs. Barron trouble.

He tipped his head to me. "I better get back to work. I need to look over the books."

And I had better go confront the possibility of bedbugs.

Yet I'd faced far, far worse in the last few days, and I'd likely face far worse in the days to come.

The cacophony of shouts, five different styles of music, and occasional gunfire filtered into the hotel.

At least none of the trouble had made it inside yet.

Agnarr strode through the hotel lobby.

The front desk clerk glanced up for a moment, then returned his attention to his novel.

A few more steps brought him to the dining room's entrance.

Two waitresses in their early twenties closed up the place—one stacking chairs on tables and the other mopping.

He braced a hand against the doorframe. "Are you ladies doing all right?"

The one stacking chairs—a girl with blonde hair and freckles—paused. "We are. Thank you for asking."

"Yell if you need something. I'll be around."

She nodded and swung a chair onto the table.

He pushed away from the doorframe and strode upstairs. Doc and Mrs. Barron had retired about an hour ago, as had Svana.

Doc Barron had griped about him working the night shift as well as the day shift, but his griping couldn't change the fact that the fellow due to work the night shift hadn't shown up.

Besides, he'd functioned on less sleep than this many times.

The hallway lay still, lit only by a couple of wall sconces.

He headed down the back stairway, toured the darkened kitchen, then returned to the lobby.

The clerk again looked up from his novel. "You're more industrious than the other guy." The clerk motioned to a cluster of chairs off to the side of the lobby. "He spends most of his time snoozing over there when Doc isn't looking."

Barron should fire the slacker.

The clerk pushed his spectacles up on his thin nose. "Doc said you're a recent exile. What'd you do?"

He'd have to get used to carefully answering questions like this. Because telling anyone he'd been captain of the royal guard was a death sentence. "I made a mistake on the job."

The clerk gave a low whistle. "Must've been some mistake. Somebody get killed?"

"No."

The fellow palmed the air. "Okay, okay. Don't get so touchy. Just trying to make conversation."

Neither of them was being paid to converse.

He gave the clerk a nod, then turned away.

The front door swung open, and a heavyset man who'd checked in during the late afternoon headed toward the staircase.

"Evening, sir."

The man scowled and trudged upstairs.

"Must've lost too much at the tables." The clerk cackled.

Couldn't he go back to his reading?

"I'm not an exile." The fellow's chair squeaked. "Nope. Lived here my whole life. My grandpappy was the exile. They threw him out of Fairrlande 'cause he shot a man dead. He claims it was justified, but he wasn't exactly an upstanding man if you know what I mean."

Apparently, the clerk's novel didn't hold his attention.

Agnarr turned enough that he had both the clerk and the front door in his peripheral. "Are you planning to go to Fairrlande when you're of age?"

The clerk scoffed. "This is all I know. What would I want with stuffy ol' Fairrlande? I've got a nice, easy job here. I've got family. Friends. You know?"

"Sure." Except he'd left his job, friends, and all family but Svana back in Fairrlande.

Mother and Father would be ashamed once they found out he'd been exiled—ashamed and grieved.

He should've gotten leave to go visit them earlier in the year. But he hadn't, and now he no longer had the chance.

Yet another mistake he'd made.

A tall, thin fellow strode into the lobby, muttering curses.

"Good evening, sir."

The man cussed louder. "Nothing good about it. That dirty Leif Havard took me for all I had."

How probable was it that there were two men by the odd name of Leif Havard?

With another string of curses, the failed gambler dragged up the stairs.

"It looks like he won't be staying here much longer." The clerk tapped an erratic beat on the front desk.

He might not be the only one. "Who is this Leif Havard?"

The clerk leaned back in his chair. "I'd steer clear of him if I were you."

It figured that the clerk would pick now to quit running his mouth.

Agnarr crossed his arms. "Why?"

The man stared at him—brow furrowed—like he thought he'd lost his mind. "He's a dangerous man. I heard he was exiled from Fairrlande for trying to assassinate one of the king's advisors."

That settled it.

"I've heard tell he's killed at least ten men since he came to Long Gulch a year ago ..."

He strode upstairs to the tune of the clerk's rambling.

Not only would Havard have it in for him if he found out he were here but he also knew he'd served the king.

If Havard didn't kill him and Svana, the townspeople would once Havard told them who he was.

He drew his room key from his pocket, knocked once on the door, then unlocked it. "We're leaving."

Chapter 3

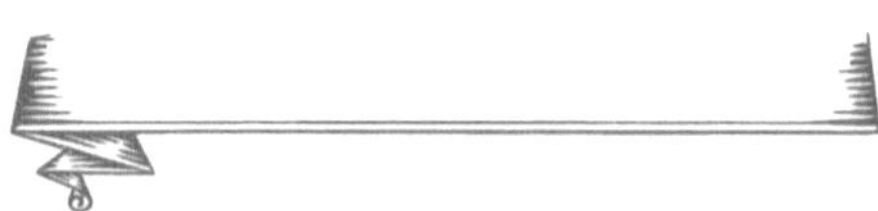

A cool, arid wind buffeted my face and tangled my hair. The canteen the Barrons had given me tapped against my hip with every step, and Agnarr loomed beside me.

At least a sliver of a moon took the edge off of the darkness suffocating the desert and cast the landscape in a blue tint.

"Who is Leif Havard?" Besides the reason we'd left Long Gulch and our jobs in the middle of the night.

Agnarr stiffened. "A criminal who had his hands in every kind of crime you can imagine."

Silence stretched between us.

For Agnarr to be sure that this man would kill us on sight—or leave it to the citizens of Long Gulch—there had to be more to the story than that.

He let out a rough breath. "He attempted to assassinate one of the king's advisors. My men and I detained him before he could get to the advisor. Which led to his exile. He vowed retribution."

"Why was he not executed?" No, execution wasn't a common form of punishment in Fairrlande—except for when it came to those who attempted to harm the king and those close to him.

"The advisor wasn't harmed and convinced the king to have mercy on Havard."

Chills ran across my arms, and I rubbed them away.

At least Agnarr hadn't come face to face with this Havard in Long Gulch.

"You think I'm a coward?"

What? I bit back the word. "No. I think … I think that you know you don't have anything to prove. That you don't feel the need to pick a fight." And risk my life.

He ran his fingers through his hair and left a disheveled mess in his wake. "I don't like running from trouble."

"I've always heard that distance is the best defense."

Not that I knew much about fighting. But that idiom had served me well when dealing with sketchy characters.

I rested my hand on his arm.

He adjusted the straps supporting the pack of supplies the Barrons had given us. "And I don't like running out on a job."

"They understood." And they also likely hadn't wanted one of Havard's targets working in their hotel.

"I didn't plan to stay in Long Gulch permanently, but I sure planned to stay there longer than that."

Laughter pressed for release. Not that his words were all that humorous or that this situation was one to laugh at.

Lack of sleep had to be affecting me.

Something hard caught my right shoe, and I pitched forward.

He grabbed my forearm, stopping my fall.

I regained my balance and limped forward, toes throbbing. "Thank you."

He let out a breath. "I couldn't take them up on the offer of horses. It would've been too much."

My near fall shouldn't make him feel guilty.

The Barrons had already given us the clothes we wore, a nightgown for me, hats, Agnarr's weapon, the canteens, the pack Agnarr carried, and enough food to last us a few days if we were careful—on top of all they'd done for us at the hotel.

He kicked a rock to the side. "I'll pay them back once I get another job."

The chills returned to my arms. "Is Dead Ridge far enough away from him?"

"No." His answer came all too quickly. "We need to make it to Clear Bend."

That meant crossing the Rykfallinn River. It seemed I couldn't escape that rickety ferry—or the beady little crocodile eyes that tracked its progress.

"You don't like Clear Bend? Doc said it was a well-established town with plenty of jobs."

Why was it that I always had to share my fears and he never did? "It's a fine town."

He could experience the crossing for himself once we got there and figured out something to barter for the ride across.

He took my hand. "Barron said there haven't been any dragon sightings in the last year."

Maybe this Havard had scared them off.

"I've only seen one in my entire life." Word was they tended to keep to the mountains along the very western edge of the wastelands. They'd never ventured as far east as where we were now.

"I don't need to see one." His chuckle was forced.

Maybe he'd like the crocodiles better.

The silence between us returned, broken only by the far-off yipping of coyotes.

Would word reach Havard that Agnarr had been in Long Gulch? And if Havard did find out that Agnarr had been there, to what lengths would he go to hunt him down?

Or was I merely borrowing worries?

Yet for Agnarr to take this threat so seriously, it had to be of great danger.

"What is he like?"

Agnarr released my hand and adjusted his pack. "Clever. Ruthless. Relentless when it serves his purposes. I thought he'd seek his revenge despite his exile, but I assume he found more profitable things to do."

Gambling, for one, Doc had said.

Yet whatever obstacle his exile had presented was now removed.

"He hasn't heard I was there."

In other words, if he had, I'd know it.

I rubbed at the persistent chills.

The night gaped around me, and the cry of some desert bird split the air.

I sidled closer to Agnarr.

His strides stretched long, and I lengthened mine to match. At least he stood only a couple of inches taller than my five foot ten.

"We'll stop and rest when the sun gets high."

Given that there wasn't a single trace of dawn on the horizon, that rest would be a long time in coming.

"Unless you need to stop before then."

Coming from almost anyone else, that would've been a challenge. Coming from Agnarr, it was only care. "I'm fine for now."

I'd had rest. I was full and hydrated. I could keep going for a few hours.

And hopefully the journey to Clear Bend would be without trouble.

Moonlight reflected off the dark, rippling waters of the Rykfallinn River.

The ferry operator's shack lay dark as well, but Barron had said the man ran the ferry at all hours.

No need to delay their journey until morning. He needed to put as much distance as possible between them and Havard.

Svana closed the distance between them, and her arm brushed his.

"What's wrong?"

She huffed a sigh. "Just watch out for crocodiles."

Crocodiles were dangerous for sure, but they didn't have Havard's malevolence.

"I'll keep an eye out for them." He started for the operator's shack.

Water lapped at the riverbank twenty or so yards ahead, but no dark, reptilian shapes crawled from the water. "They're not going to bother us as long as we leave them alone."

Unlike Havard.

She strode along beside him. "I just don't like how they watch the ferry. It's almost like they're waiting for someone to fall off."

"I won't let you fall off."

She gave a light laugh. "My balance isn't that bad. I hope."

He stopped in front of the shack and knocked on the door.

Cursing sounded from inside. "I'm coming. I'm coming. Don't be in such a hurry."

He slid his hand into his pocket, and the silver coins Mrs. Barron had hidden in the pack when he wasn't looking brushed his fingers.

It'd save the trouble of bartering, but she shouldn't have done that. It was just one more thing he'd have to repay.

Lantern light flared through the cracks in the door, then the door swung open to reveal a stoop-shouldered fellow with a gray beard straggling to his belt. "You want across?"

Why else would he have knocked on this fellow's door?

The man hobbled from the shack and slammed the door behind him. "It's gonna cost ya."

Agnarr tossed him a silver coin. "Let's get on with it."

The fellow grinned, light from the lantern he held showing a few black gaps where teeth should've been. He handed the lantern to Svana. "You can be in charge of the light, lady."

Agnarr fell into step behind the operator, then helped Svana onto the collection of boards masquerading as a ferry.

He stepped on behind her and tugged her down beside him on a bench that'd seen better days.

The thing had better hold together until they got across. Because Svana had been right. At least ten pairs of eyes glowed from the river.

The operator untied the ferry, poled it out into the river, and cackled. "Don't ya worry. I've only lost a couple passengers."

"Comforting." Svana's mumble was for his ears alone.

"That's a couple too many."

The fellow laughed again, poling them farther into the river.

The crocodiles drifted along beside them.

"You like them?" Svana's voice was nothing but a whisper.

"What's not to like? We're in the boat. They're in the water."

She set the lantern beside her on the bench. "I appreciate them as one of God's creations, but I don't want to be up close and personal with one."

The operator laughed. "Like I said, only two of my passengers have gotten too close to them. It wasn't a pretty sight."

That wasn't what Svana needed to hear. "Thanks for taking us across."

The man jerked a nod. "You ain't from around here."

That was no question. What Svana had told him was a Fairrlandian accent must be obvious to the operator. Then again, a lot of the residents of the wastelands bore a Fairrlandian accent.

"A recent exile." The man smirked at him.

"Yes." At least the approach of the ferry to the opposite bank would cut off any further questioning.

When the ferry reached the other side, he helped Svana off.

The bank stood empty of crocodiles. Svana should be pleased.

Except she glanced around like one would arise from the muddy ground and charge at her.

She should be back in Fairrlande in their comfortable house. Not out here trudging through the desert.

He half-turned. The ferry retreated to the other side of the river, the lantern pushing aside the darkness. "If we keep a good pace, we should reach Clear Bend by midmorning."

Surely that would be enough of a barrier between them and Havard. At least until he saved some money.

Havard had plenty to occupy his attention. Besides, Havard had no reason to suspect he'd been exiled as well. He'd told only the Barrons his full name, and they'd promised their silence.

"You're worrying." Svana's observation wrapped around him.

"Not worrying so much as thinking."

A cold wind sliced through his shirt, carrying the muddy scent of the river. The green vegetation encouraged by the river gave way to the scrubby plants that occupied much of the desert.

He swallowed, throat as gritty as the ground. "From what Doc said, Havard rarely leaves Long Gulch."

"That's good."

In a way. But a man like Havard always had too many connections.

Still, Havard wasn't searching for him.

And he didn't need to worry Svana. "We'll take precautions so that he doesn't find us."

The wind slapped her hair in her face, and she pushed the wild strands behind her ears. "It's not abnormal for people to withhold their surnames out here."

That would be a way to further throw Havard off their trail before he was ever on it.

Please give me wisdom. And please protect us.

I pushed aside the flap and entered the tent Agnarr had purchased with the money Mrs. Barron had given us, the scent of grease clinging to my hair and waitress uniform.

Heaviness meandered through my muscles, and my feet throbbed in time with my pulse.

Two days of taking orders and running food in the busiest restaurant I'd ever seen would do that.

After setting down the sack of leftovers I'd been invited to take home, I dropped onto the blanket masquerading as our bed, grease aroma and all, and fumbled for the box of matches and the candle.

The match flared to life, and I touched it to the candle's wick. Warm, yellow light commanded the tent.

Agnarr should be home—if I could call this tent such a thing—soon from his job as a guard at the bank. From what he'd told me, the bank was guarded at all hours due to the crime that pervaded Clear Bend and the rest of the wastelands.

The thrum of piano music from the saloons and dance halls swirled through the tent, as did laughter and the occasional shout. At least there'd been no shooting tonight, and the majority of the customers had treated me respectfully.

Now if only Agnarr would come home.

And if only he'd have chosen a safer line of work.

Then again, guarding was what he knew best.

A rustling sounded outside the tent, and tension wound through me.

I slipped my hand into my skirt pocket and closed my fingers around the canister of pepper spray Agnarr had purchased with the last of the Barrons' money.

It had been my weapon of choice back when I lived out here before, and I could handle it far better than I could a derringer or dagger.

The rustling faded, and I hissed out a breath.

It'd likely just been someone getting into his tent. After all, we'd pitched ours in a veritable colony of tents given that Clear Bend's construction hadn't quite caught up to its booming population—and given that we didn't have funds to spare for a hotel room or rental house.

Footsteps thudded outside, and I again tensed.

"Svana. It's me."

Good.

I pushed to my feet and eased back the tent flap.

Agnarr ducked inside. "I don't like you being out here alone."

Me either. But what could we do about it? He had to work.

I returned to the blanket and opened the sack of leftovers. "Are you hungry?"

He tossed his hat into the corner of the tent and lowered himself to the ground. "Starving."

The biscuits I'd sent with him for lunch must've not been enough.

I drew four baked potatoes, six old rolls, and a stack of stale cookies from the sack and set them on the crate that served as our table. "I was thinking we could save the rolls and cookies for breakfast and your lunch. I'm afraid the potatoes would spoil before then."

And the last thing either of us needed was a case of food poisoning.

"Fine with me." He accepted the potato I extended to him, then bowed his head. "Thank You for this food, Lord. Thank You for providing for us. In Jesus' Name I pray. Amen."

I blinked open my eyes and took a bite of baked potato. "It needs butter and salt. And cheese."

He swallowed and shot me a weary grin. "It tastes just fine to me."

Hunger must've desensitized his taste buds. "Everything went well today?"

"Just fine."

Unlike yesterday when he'd had to wrangle a drunk customer from the bank. Not that such a thing fazed him.

And on any given day, something worse could happen.

Not a thought I needed invading my mind when I was taking people's orders and dealing with their complaints.

He finished off his potato and reached for another one. "Yours?"

"I didn't dump anyone's food on them." Even if at least a couple of customers had deserved as much.

"The owner's treating you well? No problem customers?"

"Yes. And there's always a problem customer or two."

He chuckled. "None really out of line?"

I shook my head, then ate the final bite of my potato. "The last one's yours."

And given that he'd consumed his second one in three or four bites, he needed it.

He lifted it from the crate. "We can split it."

"I may or may not have sampled a piece of cake on one of my breaks."

He ran a hand through his hair, and a few strands stuck straight up.

I reached over to smooth them down.

His features softened.

"No, thank you." I grinned. "There will be no kissing while you're still eating that potato."

He inhaled the thing in two bites, then leaned toward me, cheeks bulging.

I ducked to the side and brushed a kiss to that bulging cheek. "I'd recommend swallowing. And please don't choke."

He swallowed and laughed. A deep belly laugh that filled the tent.

Our marriage might have started out on rather desperate terms and quickly been thrown into the fire of exile, but we were here. We were surviving.

A testament to the grace of God.

He again leaned toward me. This time, he touched his lips to mine.

All too soon, he eased back. "You smell like you've been swimming in grease."

I fanned my hand in front of my face. "Such a charming compliment. I could just swoon."

More likely I'd just get dizzy because of my own scent.

He laughed, the skin at the corners of his eyes crinkling.

And I laughed along with him. Laughed harder than I had since we'd been exiled.

"It's rather slow for a Monday morning." The bank teller adjusted one of the pins holding up her gray hair and winced.

Slow was a lot better than an attempted robbery or anything of that nature.

He braced his shoulders against the wall. "I bet it'll pick up soon."

Things seemed like they always did—and they tended to bring trouble.

She lowered her hand from her head. "I rather hope not. As you can see, I'm the only teller scheduled today, and I'm not very fast. This is only my second week working here."

"You'll do fine."

But as long as her slowness didn't make any of the customers unruly, it wasn't his problem.

"I hope so." She leaned against the front of the counter.

The bank manager should've scheduled a more experienced teller to work alongside her in case things got busy. Then again, this wasn't his bank to run.

"You'll do fine." Even if she struggled, she'd learn and get faster.

She cast a skeptical eye at him. "Or I shall enlist you to be the teller, and I shall stand guard."

"You'd do a better job than I would with all that teller business."

She studied him through narrowed eyes. "I don't know about that. You're likely a rather smart young man. But I suppose you make a more intimidating-looking guard than I would."

He allowed a brief laugh. "That's why they hired me." That and his ability to handle himself and a weapon.

"Do you have experience with that sort of thing?"

Here came the questions. "Yeah. My last position was guarding a hotel."

She gave a decisive nod. "And did anything untoward happen at that hotel while you were standing guard?"

"No." She likely wouldn't be impressed by the length of time he'd guarded the hotel though.

She smiled, and wrinkles fanned from her eyes. "Then I shall take comfort in knowing I'm safe."

"To the best of my ability, ma'am."

She returned to her station behind the counter. "You worked in a similar industry before your exile?"

She was too persistent. But at least she didn't have Svana's perception. "Yes."

She could take the hint and leave it at that.

"Oh?" Even though the bars around the counter shielded some of her expression, they couldn't erase the curiosity from her voice.

He should be better about deflecting questions by now. Yet he couldn't very well be brusque with an older lady. She wasn't one of the men he'd once commanded. And the root of the reason she asked was so she'd feel safe while doing her job. "Everything untoward that happened there was stopped before harm could come." By the grace of God.

"Good." A tinge of relief echoed through the word. "You must excuse me. I'm a nosy old lady."

That was the truth.

Two customers—both businessmen given the suits they wore—entered to the jingle of the bell hanging on the door.

One of them, an older fellow with a close-cropped gray beard and spectacles, glanced at him, offered a nod, then looked away.

The teller—unlike she'd feared—took care of them and sent them on their way in under five minutes.

The bell slapped the door upon their departure, and the teller gusted a sigh. "I shouldn't be so nervous."

He'd been hired to guard the bank. Not to provide moral support for apprehensive employees.

A random person off the street would be more comforting than he would.

"You did good."

She came around the counter and resumed her position leaning up against it. A sheen of sweat slicked her forehead, and her cheeks were flushed. "I get so flustered."

"You'll get used to it." Yep, anybody would be more comforting than he was.

She waved her hand in front of her face. "Maybe in twenty years. I should never have listened to my sister-in-law. I was bored rattling around in that old house all by myself, but being bored is a lot better than being stressed and overwhelmed."

How did one little old lady contain so many words? "Give it a few more days. I reckon you'll get used to it."

One of her eyebrows crept high. "Now you're sounding like my sister-in-law."

He shrugged. "I've been called worse."

She descended into laughter. "You haven't met my sister-in-law."

He chuckled. She had a point.

She tugged at one of the frills on her cuff. "I was over at the restaurant for breakfast this morning, and there's this new waitress there. A beautiful woman."

That was Svana.

"I heard tell that she used to be a gambler. I find that fascinating, don't you? Everyone's talking about her."

That wasn't good. The less attention they drew, the better.

Then again, unless the Barrons had developed loose lips, Havard didn't know he was married to Svana.

Still, talk spread all too fast in a town like this.

He lifted his hat and ran his fingers through hair that needed a washing. "Better not to listen to rumors."

She grinned. "Oh, where's the fun in that? Maybe I should've been a gambler instead of a teller."

"I wouldn't recommend it." Her expression revealed too many of her emotions.

She swatted at the air. "You ruin all my fun. You're too young to be such a spoilsport."

How young did she think he was? But Granny had always said when a person reached a certain age everybody beneath them looked a whole lot younger than they were.

She raised that eyebrow again. "I'll be listening for rumors about you. I can tell you're keeping secrets, young man."

Chapter 4

If one more customer silently extended a coffee mug toward me in demand of a refill, I was going to scream.

Or dump hot coffee down the back of the offending party's shirt.

I poured the steaming black liquid into the current offender's mug. He retracted it and stared straight ahead like I didn't exist.

I pasted a smile to my lips—not that the customer would see it—and continued around the dining room, filling mug after mug until the oversized coffee pot ran dry.

With quick steps, I retreated to the kitchen.

Venla, the owner and head chef, bustled past me, her round cheeks red and streaked with sweat. "You've got orders up. Tables seven and fifteen. Don't dawdle."

I'd been hustling since five o'clock this morning. But that wasn't something I could say to my boss if I wanted to keep my job. And I very much needed to keep this job.

I hurried to the window, collected both tables' orders, and delivered them.

A few customers had cleared out, and none had yet taken their places. Maybe the breakfast rush was finally slowing down.

I strode in the direction of the kitchen.

A hand brushed my arm, and I whirled around.

"Svana, Svana." Pier Nerney's drawl hadn't changed a bit. Neither had the flashy gold of his waistcoat and the outdated ruffles spilling from the front of his shirt. "What are you doing waiting tables?"

Since when was he awake before noon? "As you can see, I'm quite busy."

Rude perhaps, but it was the truth. And he would only question me more about my position here.

"Too busy to catch up with an old friend?" He smoothed his goatee.

Former competition was more like it.

He adjusted his black frock coat, and the pearly white of his pistol's grip flashed from his shoulder holster.

Legend had it he'd gunned down countless men with that weapon, but legends didn't often take notice of the truth.

I pressed my lips into yet another smile. "Maybe another time."

Venla hustled by me. "You're due for a break as it is."

Pier shot her a wink.

Of course he would have her wrapped around his little finger.

I sighed. "Let's at least move out of everyone's way." I stepped over to the wall.

He followed me and leaned his shoulder against the whitewashed wall. "I never expected to see you back here."

I lifted one shoulder. "Things change. I'm married now." Best to tell him that up front so he wouldn't start the obnoxious flirting that must've worked on Venla. "There was an ... incident, and my husband and I were exiled."

He studied me, one eyebrow raised. "You can pick up right where you left off. Everyone would be glad to have you back."

This time around, I would tell that He'd changed me. "I'm living a different life now. A new life."

He laughed. "Don't tell me you've become one of them."

"Jesus saved me."

He palmed the air. "Then surely He wouldn't mind you doing what makes you the best money." He shook his head. "You'd rather work in this place? No offense to Venla of course, but it'd take you a month to make what you'd rake in during a night at the tables."

Truth. Truth I wouldn't listen to. Even if it would be all too easy.

"It's just a game. A very profitable game if you're lucky." He stared at me like I'd lost my mind.

I swiped at a bead of sweat that was dribbling down my cheek. "I was a greedy wretch. I didn't care what I had to do to make that money. Cheat. Lie. Steal. Flirt with every man that walked in the door."

"Aw, that's not so bad. I'm sure they enjoyed it." He grinned. "I shall continue to be a greedy heathen, but I won't try to change your mind." He motioned to the customers. "I'll let them do it for me. Give this a couple of months, and you'll be right back at the tables with a few shots of whiskey to improve your mood."

Lovely. He thought I was moody. "Didn't your mother teach you better than to tell a lady that?"

His grin broadened. "Nope. She taught me how to cheat and not let anyone catch me doing it."

The same as my parents had—only they hadn't been able to cheat the fever that'd taken their lives the month before I'd turned eighteen.

I waved my hand to the sitting area much as he had a moment ago. "How about I take your order?"

"Trying to get rid of me already?" He shot me an obnoxious, toothy grin.

I again motioned to the tables and chairs. "Yes."

Not only had this conversation gone on long enough but I also had a job to do. And whatever pull Pier had with Venla could only go so far.

Somehow, that grin of his widened even more.

Oh, now he was just trying to annoy me.

But he sauntered away with a glance over his shoulder. "I'll have my regular."

One of those customers. The kind that assumed a new waitress knew his order.

And that meant I'd have to bother Venla or one of the other waitresses.

This day could only get better.

Light spilled from the saloons and cut through the darkness that blanketed Clear Bend.

Agnarr lengthened his stride and hung a right.

No reason to let Svana sit alone in that tent any longer than was necessary.

Shadowy figures stumbled from a saloon, each of them bellowing a different off-key song.

One started toward him, waving an uncoordinated fist in the air.

Not tonight. Not any night.

He half-turned toward the fellow. "Don't try it." The tone he'd used to employ on slacking members of the royal guard.

The man stumbled to a stop and lowered his fist, swaying on his feet.

His friends descended into a cacophony of laughter.

Agnarr strode on.

The saloons gave way to darkened businesses, then the businesses surrendered to a sea of tents.

He stilled in front of the fifth tent from the end. Candlelight glowed from within, and Svana's shadowed form sat still.

"Svana. It's me." He pushed aside the flap and ducked inside.

She offered him a smile. "I recognized your steps."

That she knew how he walked had to be a good sign.

He tossed his hat into the corner and lowered himself to the ground. "Your day went well?"

She opened a paper bag and pulled out a sandwich. "Well enough." She handed the sandwich to him, the movement slow.

Either she was tired from a long day or that was one bad sandwich.

He turned it over in his hands. Sure, the bread crunched a little beneath his fingers, but the aroma of roast beef filled his nose.

He raised an eyebrow. "What's wrong with it?"

She blinked at him. "Nothing. They're from yesterday—which is why I was allowed to take them home—but I ate one before I left. It was good."

Then she was tired.

Or maybe he'd read too much into one motion.

She gestured at him. "Like I said, I ate at work, so you can start eating whenever you're ready."

Thanks for this food, Lord. He took a bite, chewed, and swallowed.

His stomach grumbled.

He met Svana's eyes and laughed. "Hope you were serious when you referred to what you brought home in the plural form."

Her lips curved up into a faint smile. "I was. There's more in there. Two more to be exact."

That smile wasn't right. "What's wrong?"

Maybe having her work at that restaurant hadn't been a good idea.

Her expression turned neutral. "Everything's fine."

No. That poker face was evidence enough. "Who bothered you?"

Because he'd wring the punk's neck.

She shook her head, gaze steady. "I said that everything's fine."

He wasn't stupid enough to fall for that when everything about her shouted otherwise.

But he couldn't very well snap at her to report what was going on like he would've with one of his men. She was his wife, and he'd treat her gently, lovingly. Yet he would still find out what was going on. "Svana, I need to know so I can protect you the way I should."

The neutrality fell away, and her eyes flashed fire. "Even you can't protect me from the wretch I was."

He took another bite of the sandwich. What had brought this on? Svana—though he hadn't known her for long—wasn't given to outbursts like that. No, she was calm, in control, and all too perceptive.

She fisted her hands, red eclipsing her cheeks. But the fire in her eyes had cooled, had been replaced by dullness. "I cheated. I swindled people out of their money. I lied. I stole. I encouraged men to lust after me so I could manipulate them. I ..."

She hung her head, and her shoulders rose and fell.

Please don't let me misspeak. "And yet you're forgiven. You're justified. Because of Jesus."

She looked up then, eyes reddened and filled with unshed tears. "Yes." She sighed. "I ... I'm sorry. I shouldn't have lost control like that. You just came home. You've got to be tired. And I acted like a little fool."

He polished off another bite of sandwich. "Don't worry about it."

First the bank teller, now Svana. He wasn't cut out for all this comforting.

She swiped her hand beneath her nose. "Someone I knew from before came into the restaurant. The conversation didn't do anything but annoy me then, but the more I thought about it, the more it started bothering me. I guess it just brought back a lot of memories, and—"

"Who? Was he rude? Threatening?"

"No. And he was just another gambler." She swatted something off of her skirt. "I shouldn't have let everything get to me. The last thing I want to do is be a burden to you."

"You're not." His voice came out a little too rough.

But she was talking nonsense.

She stared at him, forehead lined like he was the one talking nonsense.

"You're not. Far, far, from it."

As well as she read him most of the time, she should know that he wasn't lying.

Yet maybe she'd convinced herself of all that nonsense too well to see clearly.

He coughed. "Look, I'm the one who got us exiled. If anyone has the right to feel bad, it's me."

"No."

She would rise to his defense and not her own.

"The king never should've exiled you for what happened. He should've punished his son."

He lifted the half-eaten sandwich. "The fact is we're out here and we've got to make the best of it. And you've been helping do that. Not being a burden."

Case closed. Nonsense put to rest.

Of all the times to not keep control of myself.

I clenched my teeth.

Agnarr lay beside me, eyes closed, hands folded behind his head.

He should've chosen a better wife, one who didn't have such a sordid past. Maybe he even wished he would've.

Not that he'd given any indication of such a thing.

He'd likely chide me for having such a thought in the first place.

Besides, having such a thought wouldn't help a thing. The fact of the matter was that he'd married me, and he wasn't the type of man to go back on his word.

Candlelight yellowed the tent's canvas.

I should get up and blow out the candle. Morning would come all too early, and I needed to try to sleep.

I eased onto my elbow and leaned toward the candle.

The distant throb of shouts filtered into the tent.

A brawl must've broken out at one of the saloons. A big one.

Agnarr stirred and grumbled something.

The shouting grew closer, louder.

Agnarr rolled to his knees and fastened his gun belt around his hips.

I fumbled for my pepper spray.

He squeezed my shoulder, then pushed back the tent flap a bit. "Not good." He lowered his hand to his side. "Get packed. I've got a bad feeling about this."

With that, he brushed aside the flap and ducked into the night.

My pulse jolted along at what had to be twice its normal speed.

From the way he talked, we'd be fleeing shortly. Again.

I pushed off our blanket into a crouched position, and shouting swirled around me.

I rolled up the blanket, tied it with two scraps of twine, and tossed it beside the pack and our canteens.

At least I hadn't changed into my nightgown yet or even taken off my shoes.

The shouts blasted my ears, and the harsher light of what had to be three or four lanterns beamed into the tent.

With a ragged breath, I blew out the candle.

"Get out of here." Enough command backed Agnarr's words to make whoever was out there think twice about whatever they had planned.

Please protect him. Please protect us.

I slung the canteens over my shoulders, jerked on the pack, and tucked the rolled-up blanket beneath my left arm.

"You dirty royal guard."

The words hit me with the force of a dozen blows.

Too many other voices took up the chant.

How had they found out? And was one of the men out there Leif Havard?

I tightened my grip on the pepper spray and untied the tent's back flap.

"You heard me. Get out of here."

Laughter. Nothing but laughter.

"Deny it. Deny that you're one of them. But we're gonna kill you just the same."

Please, Lord, please get us out of this mess.

I stepped through the tent's back flap and crouched low behind the flimsy canvas structure.

Better to be outside the fire trap in case a member of that irrational mob tossed a lantern onto it.

"You're not killing anybody. Get back." Somehow, Agnarr still maintained calm.

The mob roared.

Yet they hadn't charged him and overtaken him. Maybe they had reservations.

If only I could create a distraction.

I forced air into my lungs and let out a scream. "Dragons! Look out!"

"Where? Where? Take cover!"

Pandemonium reigned in the panicked shouts, in the trample of footsteps.

Two men darted past me in a mad race toward town.

A hand clenched my arm and jerked me to my feet. "Come on."

I raced beside Agnarr, each stride carrying me farther into the desert land surrounding Clear Bend.

My skirt tangled around my legs. My breath came in gasps. Burning flooded my lungs, and a stabbing stitch tormented my side.

I jerked my head over my shoulder.

No shadowy figures dashed after us.

I stumbled, but Agnarr's grip on my arm kept me upright.

Stride after stride. Breath after fiery breath.

Then Agnarr pulled me to a stop and pushed me behind a cluster of boulders.

I sank to the sandy ground and heaved in rasping breaths.

We'd made it. By the grace of God, we'd made it.

Despite my deception.

Something in my chest squeezed hard and tight.

Forgive me.

Maybe there'd been another way. Maybe I could've used a different method of distraction. Maybe I should've let Agnarr scare them off or talk some sense into them. Maybe—

He tugged the pack off my shoulders and slipped it on his own. "Are you all right?"

He should have the decency to sound more winded than that.

I panted until my breathing finally slowed. "Yes. Please tell me you are too."

"I've been through worse."

That I didn't need to know.

He peered around the edge of the boulder, his form cloaked in shadows. "Still clear."

Thankfully.

"There weren't really any dragons." My voice came out as a shaky mess.

He reached over and rested his hand on my shoulder. "I know."

I dropped the rolled-up blanket to the ground. "This is becoming too much of a habit."

Leaving our new jobs. Fleeing into the night.

He grunted a laugh. "Next time, I'm getting a job with a rancher. I've had enough of being in those towns."

"You know how to work with cattle and horses?" The trembling that'd been tormenting my body slacked off and left weakness in its place.

He moved his hand from my shoulder, still looking beyond that boulder. "Not well enough to get hired on at a big operation, but I'm a decent cook."

Why was I just now finding that out?

"What other secrets are you keeping?"

He only chuckled.

How could he laugh after what had almost happened? Then again, how could I even think about cooking right now?

"How did they find out you were a royal guard?"

Silence settled in, and the seconds slipped by.

He shifted, sand crunching beneath his boots. "I don't know. I didn't see anybody who would've recognized me."

And even if somebody had thought he looked familiar, they surely wouldn't have expected for the captain of the royal guard to have been exiled. Besides, Agnarr hadn't shaved since we'd been exiled. And the supposed leader of the angry mob had made no mention of Agnarr being captain of the royal guard. He'd only said he was a royal guard.

Agnarr cleared his throat. "My best guess is that it was just a rumor and they ran with it. Doesn't really matter. We'll just lay lower than we've already been doing."

Chills rippled across my skin.

Yes. We'd lay lower and hope Havard didn't hear anything that made him suspicious.

Morning sunlight beamed into his eyes and fried his face.

Too bad he hadn't thought to grab his hat before he confronted that mob. But being sunburned was far better than being killed.

Svana kept pace with him, her nose and forehead as red as his likely were.

He took a swig from his half-empty canteen. They'd need to find water sooner rather than later. "We'll stop and rest when the sun gets too high." Then they'd travel again during the evening hours and sleep at night. Given that there weren't any pressing dangers trailing them, traveling at night was an unnecessary risk.

Waves of heat shimmered ahead, toying with the scrubby desert brush and the scattered boulders, and sheer cliffs rose up to the right. Cliffs that offered a good bit of shade.

"Let's head over that way." He started toward the cliffs.

If he could find an overhang, they could wait out the hottest hours there.

Svana picked her way around a particularly rough cluster of rocks. "From what I can remember, the river we crossed on the ferry loops back around a few miles ahead—only it's supposedly shallow enough most of the time that travelers can cross it on foot."

Good. They could refill the canteens there.

Svana stumbled.

He grasped her arm to steady her. "Are you okay?"

She shot him a smile. "I'm just clumsy. I think it was a rock."

He gave her arm a squeeze, then released it. "You're a trooper."

And it was a good thing she was. If she'd been a whiner, these last few days would've been a whole lot worse.

"Oh, I don't know about that." She took a sip from her canteen. "I just didn't see any other option. Complaining takes a lot of energy."

He stepped into the shade offered by the cliffs, and the temperature took a dive.

"That feels so good." She let out a satisfied sigh.

It'd at least save them from a worse sunburn. "Be on the lookout for an overhang or cave."

"You'd like to spend some time with rattlers?"

Better rattlers than an angry mob. "I'll check things out before you go in."

"I'm not afraid of them. They don't watch me like those crocodiles do."

A rattler could be just as deadly as a crocodile.

A crevice split the cliff several yards ahead.

Svana shook her head. "That's too small."

"I'll check it out. It might widen farther back."

She eyed him like he might've lost his mind.

He held back a grin. "I'll check it out."

A man stepped from the crevice. "No you won't."

Agnarr jumped in front of Svana and reached for his gun.

A revolver materialized in the man's hand. "Don't do it."

Agnarr lifted his hands. "Nobody's doing anything. We were just looking for shelter."

The man appraised him with hard gray eyes. Given the fellow's dusty, worn clothing and the unkempt state of his black beard and hair, he'd been out here for a while.

Either a bandit or a man running from something.

Neither was a good option.

If de-escalating the situation didn't work, he'd have to get in close and gain control of the man's gun. Or draw his own weapon without getting filled with lead.

Svana's hands pressed against his back.

Please give me wisdom.

"We'll be leaving now."

The man narrowed his eyes, his gun as steady as ever.

Agnarr took a slow step back, and Svana's shoes rasped against sand and rock behind him. "Put the gun away. We're no danger to you."

"Stop." The fellow's voice held a rough edge. "You were hunting me."

For sure, he'd have to come across a crazy in this place. "No. I was looking for a place to get out of the sun. Like I said, we'll be on our way."

Svana's hands trembled against his back.

The man cocked his head, then laughed. "Agnarr Vev, is that you?"

Leave it to the crazy to recognize him. Better not to acknowledge what he'd said. "Put that gun away. We're leaving."

"It is you, Agnarr." With a laugh, the fellow holstered his revolver.

Wait. Behind that beard and mess of hair was Branek Renatus.

"What're you doing out here?" He stepped toward Branek, shook his hand, and slapped him on the back.

To think they'd both wound up in the Rykfallinn Wastelands. Seemed neither of their plans had worked out.

But Branek was running—or hiding—from something. That much was obvious.

Until he found out what was going on, he'd better keep his guard up.

"What are you doing out here?"

Branek gave a poor imitation of a smile. "Living."

"You've gotten awful fast with that gun." Seemed all those years of practice had paid off.

Branek's eyes hardened. "Seems that way."

Childhood friend or not, something had changed about Branek. Something that bore watching.

"Agnarr?" Svana's voice filtered from behind him. "You know him?"

He motioned her to his side. "Svana, this is Branek Renatus. We grew up together. Lost contact when I entered the royal guard." He nodded to Branek. "Branek, this is my wife, Svana."

Branek tugged off his hat and dipped his head. "A pleasure to meet you, ma'am." He glanced up and grinned. "My apologies on being saddled with him."

Svana laughed. "It's good to meet you as well."

Branek shifted his gaze between the two of them. "Never thought you'd be one to be exiled."

Branek must've been exiled as well. He wouldn't have come to the wastelands of his own accord—unless he was running from the Fairrlande law.

"Did you cross the king?"

"Something like that." The sorry tale didn't need to be rehashed. "What's this about someone hunting you?"

Branek shrugged. "Long story."

Or an incriminating one.

"Why don't you come inside?" Branek nodded to the crevice. "You look like you've been traveling a ways."

Without another word, the man turned his back and stepped into the crevice.

Turning his back to them said he trusted them, yet Branek hadn't proved himself trustworthy yet.

"Agnarr?" Svana studied him, eyebrows raised in question.

"Stay close to me." He strode through the crack in the cliff. *Please give me wisdom.*

After he'd taken a few steps, the crevice widened.

Branek stood beside another opening in the rock. "Watch your step."

Agnarr followed Branek through the chiseled doorway and down four flights of stone steps, torches at regular intervals lighting the way. The staircase spilled into an oval cavern also lit by torches.

"What is this place?" Svana's voice came strained.

Understandable for a woman who wasn't fond of mines.

Branek rested his hands on his hips. "Best I can tell, a tribe or something lived down here."

A rough table and a chair stood by the rock wall, and several openings led from the cavern.

The faint rush of fast-moving water echoed through the cavern. "You've got a river down here?"

Branek grabbed a torch from the holder on the wall and strode to one of the doorways. "I'll show you."

For whatever reason Branek had hidden himself away like this, he'd sure picked a good place to do it.

Agnarr shrugged out of the pack and lowered it to the ground along with his canteen. Svana did the same with her canteen. The rolled-up blanket he'd fastened to the top of the pack canted to the right.

"Coming?" Branek cocked his head.

"Yep." He fell into step behind Branek.

The doorway led into a tunnel lined with various darkened rooms or tunnels.

A man could get lost down here a little too easily.

Svana's footsteps echoed behind him.

He glanced over his shoulder. "You okay?"

She let out a shaky breath. "I like the cooler temperature, but ..."

Branek chuckled. "It takes some getting used to. I've been here almost a year and still haven't explored it all."

"That's not comforting." Svana's words were nothing but a mumble.

He again tilted his head over his shoulder. "If you need to go back up, just say the word."

"Like I said, I'm enjoying the cool."

The tunnel opened up into another cavern, this one split in two by a swift-moving river.

Branek stilled on the bank, light from his torch reflecting on the water.

Fish—some close to four feet long and so pale they were almost translucent—darted beneath the surface.

Svana crouched on the edge of the bank, cupped her hands in the water, and drank handful after handful.

"They're good eating." Branek gestured at the fish. "I've got one cooking for lunch."

The man had a lot of explaining to do. "You've been living down here for a year surviving on fish?"

Branek secured the torch in a holder fastened to the rock and leaned against the wall. "Them, whatever I can hunt and gather topside, and cave vegetables."

"Cave vegetables?" Svana pushed to her feet and stared at Branek like he'd grown a second head.

Maybe the man had lost his mind living down here alone for a year.

"Sure." Branek grinned, looking a lot closer to the eighteen-year-old kid he'd been the last time he'd seen him. "Cave cabbage, cave carrots, cave potatoes."

Svana swiped her hands on her skirt and left damp streaks behind. "Vegetables need sunlight to grow."

If anything, Branek's grin widened. "These don't." He raised his hands. "Don't ask me. I don't understand it. But they're as pale and freaky-looking as those fish."

Maybe he had heatstroke and was hallucinating all of this.

He knelt beside the river, plunged his hands into water the temperature of glacial run-off, and splashed it onto his face. The icy liquid sucked the heat from his sunburn, and chills claimed his skin.

Yeah, not a hallucination.

He shoved to his feet and faced Branek. "You've got some explaining to do."

Branek gave a slow, almost hesitant nod. "After we get some of that fish into us."

Chapter 5

Agnarr forked the final bite of fish and strangely translucent potatoes into his mouth.

Svana—who sat in the lone chair at the table—set her fork down and smiled. "That was delicious."

Branek acknowledged the compliment with a nod. "Glad you liked it."

Agnarr grinned. "Anything would taste good after wandering around in that desert." Couldn't let the man get a bigger head than he already had.

"May I help clean up?" Svana stood, plate and cup in hand.

Branek shook his head. "I've got it. But thanks for offering."

Enough of this small talk. Branek had plenty of explaining to do.

He raised an eyebrow at the man.

Branek looked away.

Figured.

Svana set her plate and cup back on the table and covered a yawn. "I know you all are planning to talk, but I'm exhausted. I don't want to be rude, but is there anywhere I can close my eyes for a few minutes?"

Depending on what Branek had to say, it might be a good thing for her to be out of the room.

"Sure." Branek set his plate on the table, then leaned back against the wall. "Any of the first three rooms on the right side of that tunnel leading to the river would work good for you."

"Thanks." She shot him a weary smile, walked over to their pack, and collected the rolled-up blanket.

Agnarr met her eyes. "Yell if you need me."

"I will." She patted her skirt pocket.

Good. She had her pepper spray.

She wandered into the tunnel.

He lowered his plate and tin cup to the table and folded his arms. "Might as well get started."

Branek scowled at him. "You've gotten pushy in your old age."

Now that was the kid he'd grown up with. The one always rubbing it in that he was the elder—by ten months.

"Came with the job."

"I figured." Branek turned his cup in his hands. "Did you make captain of the guard?"

He answered the question with a nod. He'd made it and lost it.

Branek let out a rough breath. "You saw how fast I am with that gun?"

"Sure." Too fast. If Branek had been intent on killing them, both he and Svana would've been fatally injured in a matter of moments.

Branek scuffed his boot against the rocky ground. "Back in Fairrlande, I was working as a quick draw performer in a Wild Wastelands show."

That was far from Branek's plan of being a sheriff.

Another scuff of his boot against the rocks. "Some idiot cornered me one night and made to draw on me. I hit his hand. Turns out he was the town mayor's son, and I ended up exiled."

"Rough." But not rough enough to turn Branek into a hermit.

Branek cupped the back of his neck and squeezed. "I made it to Long Gulch just fine. Got a job and everything. But some gunfighter learned who I was and confronted me. Turns out he's some kind of legend out here, and I outdrew him."

That's what he meant when he'd asked if Agnarr was hunting him. "And now every two-bit gunfighter in the wastelands wants his shot at you."

Branek gave a slow nod. "I've gone from town to town. Changed my name a few times. Grown a beard. But there's always somebody who finds me. So I came out here. I'm not a killer." He let out a rough laugh. "What were you expecting me to say? That I'm some kind of criminal?"

Well, he hadn't been much of a friend. But he couldn't put Svana at risk by being overly trusting either.

"Something like that."

Branek chuckled and slapped his leg. "Good one."

He laughed along with him. "You've got a good setup down here. How do you keep those torches burning?" From the way Branek talked, there was no way he was traveling to town for supplies.

Branek glanced to one of the torches burning on the wall. "The handle is made from a type of wood that's fireproof, and the fuel comes from a combustible cactus. They'll burn for about a day before I have to dip them again."

Good to know.

Branek pushed away from the wall and set his cup on the table. "You and Svana are welcome to stay here as long as you need. Whatever trouble you're trying to keep ahead of won't find you here."

"As far as I can tell, we're not being pursued." He scratched his beard. "The townspeople of Clear Bend didn't take kindly to assuming I was a royal guard."

Branek winced. "That'd do it. Glad you got out of there without too much trouble."

"Yep." And that trouble—or more like it—had better not find them here.

"I'm getting up." Agnarr rested his hand on my shoulder. "But you should sleep in."

I forced my eyes open.

Darkness no longer pressed over the rock-enclosed room where we'd spent the night. No, inch-wide trails of blue light crisscrossed the walls.

I blinked. "What is that?"

Agnarr sat up, pulling the blanket away from me in the process.

Cool, damp air that reeked of all things cave washed over me.

I tugged the blanket back into place. "What caused that?"

"Foot-long glowing slugs. I've been watching them for the past hour or so."

The pale blue light that radiated from what had to be their trails was beautiful. The fact that they'd been crawling all over the walls while I slept, however, was not.

"How interesting." I pulled the blanket to my chin.

At least the blanket—or the floor—wasn't covered in glowing trails.

"They won't hurt you." He fastened his gun belt around his hips and straightened his shirt. "Really. Get some more sleep."

Somehow, I'd managed to sleep last night despite the tons of rocks hovering over my head. But Branek had lived here for a year and hadn't met the horrible fate of a collapse.

I would just have to control my fear so I could pretend to be the trooper Agnarr thought I was.

I pressed my eyes shut.

Agnarr's footfalls echoed against stone, then his and Branek's voices rang through the cave.

Just over a week ago, I'd been a newlywed living in a comfortable house in Fairrlande waiting for my husband to return home. Now, I was a newlywed exile sleeping in a room occupied by gigantic, glowing slugs.

Life could change a little too quickly.

Yet I'd learned long ago to roll with the punches.

The voices dissipated, and fog drifted into my mind.

"Svana." Agnarr's voice blasted through the room.

"What time is it?" I jolted to my feet, the blanket puddling around me. Harsh golden torchlight had replaced the slugs' trails, courtesy of Agnarr standing in the doorway with a torch in hand.

"Two hours after noon. Branek found a woman while he was above. She's overheated and dehydrated. You need to look after her."

I raked my fingers through my tangled hair. At least I hadn't changed into my nightgown last night. "Of course. Where is she?"

"Right next door."

I hurried from the room and ducked into a similar room lit by yet another torch.

A still woman lay on a blanket, her face bright red, her clothes dusty. Branek stood by the wall, features tight and pale above his beard.

Please help me care for her the way I should.

I brushed my hands down my skirt, then knelt beside the woman. "I'll need fresh water, water with a pinch of salt, and some cloths. And my nightgown for her to wear."

Both Agnarr and Branek strode from the room.

Within moments, Branek set a bowl, a cup, a pitcher of water, and a small pile of rags beside me. Agnarr tossed me my nightgown.

"Thank you."

Both men vacated the room like I'd shooed them out.

"They left rather quickly." Even if she couldn't talk back right now, I could keep up a conversation.

The woman blinked at me, her blue eyes glazed.

I urged my lips into a smile. "Maybe you intimidated them. How about some water?"

I lifted her head and helped her take a few small sips. "That's enough for now." I eased her head back to the blanket.

I'd need to see about finding something that could serve as a pillow once I'd gotten her comfortable.

Her eyes fluttered shut.

"I'm going to get you out of those dusty, hot clothes and sponge you off with some cool water. That should feel good."

Talking to someone who didn't speak back was rather odd. Yet if I were in her position, I'd want to know what was going on.

Once I'd gotten her out of her clothes and shoes, I cleaned her off and helped her into my nightgown. "That feels better, doesn't it?"

Her eyes slid open, and she stared me down.

"More water?" After lifting her head, I held the cup to her cracked and bleeding lips. "That's good. You'll be feeling better in no time."

Had she been traveling with a group that'd been attacked? Had she run away from home for some reason? Was she fleeing some type of danger?

I wet three cloths, squeezed them out, and settled them on her forehead and wrists.

Those, along with the cave's temperature, would help her cool down.

And I'd keep getting water into her.

"I should've introduced myself earlier. I'm Svana."

The woman's lips parted, and she whispered something.

I helped her drink a little more water. "What was that? I couldn't quite make out what you said."

"Eldina." Her ragged whisper bounced off the walls.

I patted her shoulder. "It's nice to meet you, Eldina. You're safe here."

Agnarr and Branek would keep away whatever danger had ended with her being lost, sunburned, and dehydrated in the desert.

"I hope so." Her eyelids flickered closed. "I ... hope ... so."

"I don't like it." Branek paced from one side of the main cavern to the other.

Agnarr slipped his hands into his pockets.

The woman hadn't been alert. It stood to reason she wouldn't remember how to get down here. Besides, Branek didn't have to interact with her, and they didn't have to tell her who he was. Unless she'd already recognized him.

"Do you know her?"

Branek came to a halt and raked his hand through his hair. "No."

Svana stepped into the cavern. "She's settled, has drunk some water, and is sleeping now."

"Good." He closed the distance between them and pushed a tangled strand of hair behind her ear. "Thanks for taking care of her."

"Yeah." Branek's voice came out rough. "Thanks, Svana." He mumbled something under his breath. "I don't like this."

Svana's features softened. "You did the right thing. You couldn't have left her out there."

Just because he'd done the right thing didn't mean there wouldn't be repercussions.

Branek shook his head. "We're going to have to find out what she's running from—because she's running from something just as sure as I'm standing here. We're going to have to figure out a solution to that problem, tend to the problem, then take her back to where she came from. Or we're going to have to find someone who has reason to take care of her and let him tend to the problem."

True enough. But the woman could give them a lot of answers—and maybe even a solution—if she woke up willing to talk.

Branek picked up his pacing again like he thought he could outrun that list he'd rattled off.

Agnarr strode to the table and leaned a hip against it. "Did she say anything when you were carrying her here?"

"She was mumbling, but I couldn't understand any of it."

Nothing helpful there. At least not anything they could make use of.

Svana tugged her hair over her shoulder. "I'm going to go sit with her. I don't want her waking up alone in a strange place."

He'd gained a kind, compassionate wife in Svana.

He gave her a nod. "Tell me when she wakes up. I have some questions for her." Yet if he asked those questions in too demanding of a way, she'd clam up for sure. And he might even scare her. "On second thought, you'd better ask them." Svana would be gentle and patient. "Ask her name, how she got out here, where she's from, who her family is. That kind of stuff."

"Okay." Svana turned toward the doorway leading into the tunnel, then glanced over her shoulder. "Her name is Eldina. She didn't give me her surname."

Suspicious. The action of a woman with something to hide.

"Then again, I only introduced myself to her using my first name. She could've been responding in kind. And she was exhausted."

Time would tell.

Branek stopped his pacing and drew a tin of something from his pocket. "Salve for her sunburn. And you two look like you could use it too."

Svana took it from him with a smile. "Thanks." Quick steps carried her into the tunnel.

"Yell if you need me."

Branek resumed his pacing.

"Calm down over there. That woman didn't look like a gunfighter to me."

But she could know one, so Branek's worries had some merit.

Branek scowled at him and stilled. "I've heard there are female gunfighters, but I've never seen one. Don't want to either. My mama raised me not to shoot women."

"Don't worry. You'd scare them off with that hair and beard of yours."

Branek's scowl deepened. "I wasn't expecting visitors."

"That's obvious." He followed the jab with a chuckle. "If you beg Svana, she might give you a haircut."

Branek's scowl turned to a grin. "That what she did to yours?"

"Hey now."

"You can dish it out, but you still can't take it."

Svana peeked her head into the cavern. "You all are echoing really loudly in her room."

Branek's grin disappeared. "Sorry about that."

Sure, the woman needed her rest, but they also needed answers. "We'll keep it down."

But Svana had already disappeared into the tunnel.

Branek braced himself against the cavern wall. "Guess I'm too used to living underground. Lost all my manners."

Agnarr swallowed a laugh that would echo for sure. "You never had them."

Branek shook his head. "I better get started on lunch. Fried cabbage and baked fish sounds decent."

"I'll go topside and take a look around." And make sure no one was trying to sneak down here on them.

"No need. I was up there not so long ago, and I strung a trip wire just inside the crevice. It's attached to a bell so we'll hear if somebody's looking around too close."

Branek had thought this through—except for one thing. "Smoke from that stove of yours is going to give us away."

"Nope." Branek gave his head a single shake. "I bought some special kind of wood off a peddler outside of Long Gulch. It stays red-hot no matter what you do to it and doesn't produce any smoke. Gotta be careful handling it for sure, but it came with a special box for safe storage and everything."

Branek was a little too proud of that wood.

Branek shrugged. "Beats having to gather wood. And having to eat cold meals when you want to avoid detection."

True.

Now if they could just get some answers from that lady.

Eldina stared at me, her eyes widened in panic.

"You're okay. You're safe here." As I'd repeated at leave four or five other times. "Would you like more water? You're cooling down nicely."

Nicely enough that I'd been able to remove the wet cloths from her head and wrists and apply the salve to her poor sunburned face.

She shook her head, her brown hair scrubbing the makeshift pillow I'd fashioned from my and Agnarr's blanket. "No. I ... I ..." She squeezed her eyes shut, and her face contorted.

I took her hand in mine. "Is something hurting you?"

Her body bore no bruises or cuts. Maybe I'd given her too much water, and it'd made her stomach cramp.

She shook her head again, the movement spastic. "Where am I? Who are you?"

"I'm Svana." I would keep my voice gentle. "A friend of my husband found you in the desert and brought you here. This is his home."

But she didn't need specifics about Branek.

She squinted up at me. "You're—you're not affiliated with them?"

She wasn't speaking of Agnarr and Branek. "The reason why you were alone in the desert." I spoke the sentence as a statement.

She blinked, and her eyes reddened. "They kidnapped me."

Horrible. Completely horrible.

"I—I managed to get away from them."

At least she seemed willing to talk.

Maybe I could gain some information that would help us determine how to help this poor woman. "Who kidnapped you?"

"I don't know." She shuddered. "There were two of them. Two big men."

I gave her hand a light squeeze. "You're safe here. They're not going to find you here."

"I know." Her voice was nothing more than a rasp. "Natives attacked and killed them. That's when I escaped. I thought they'd kill me too, but they let me go."

Thank You for protecting her.

I offered her a smile. "We'll help you get back home. Where are you from?"

"Long Gulch."

She was a long way from home.

"You have family there?"

She dipped her head in a tentative nod. "Yes."

"What are their names? We can help you contact them, and they can pick you up in the nearest town."

Something in her expression shifted. "I—I think it'd be better if I didn't tell you. You see, my—my family has a lot of enemies."

Her kidnapping was proof enough of that.

"Many families in Long Gulch have a lot of enemies."

She closed her eyes. "My head hurts, and I'd like to sleep."

Pushing her right now would gain me nothing.

I curled my fingers around the half-full cup of water. "You should drink a little more before you rest."

"That would be nice."

I lifted her head from the pillow, and she drained the cup.

"There you go. Get some more rest. That and water are the best things for you right now. And when you wake up, I imagine there will be some lunch ready."

And given the smells of baking fish and frying cabbage, lunch was well on its way.

My stomach rumbled.

Eldina's lips quirked up in the slightest. "Thank you. For taking care of me."

"Of course. You'll be feeling back to normal in no time."

In fact, she'd already made a good recovery given what she'd been through.

"I'll be praying for you."

"Thank you." Her features relaxed. "I'm not too religious myself, but I don't figure such a thing can hurt. I know my mama prays for me all the time."

Something in my stomach clenched. If only my mother had been the praying sort. "Then you've got two of us praying for you."

Her breathing deepened and grew even.

After a few minutes, I eased to my feet and headed into the main cavern.

Both Agnarr and Branek leaned against the wall.

"I assume you heard everything she said." After all, this cave carried sound quite well, and they had eavesdropping written all over their faces.

Agnarr grinned at Branek. "See what I have to put up with? She can tell what I've been doing a little too easily."

I laughed. "Only a guilty man would have a problem with that."

"Good one." Branek gave a single clap, then winced.

He and Agnarr must have been complete terrors when they were growing up.

"We'll speak quietly so we don't wake her and so she doesn't hear us." Agnarr pushed away from the wall. "Unless she decides to tell who her family is, the best way to handle this is to get her to the nearest town once she feels up to traveling and let her contact her family from there. Both Svana and I will accompany her to keep things proper."

An honorable plan even though many residents of the wastelands couldn't care less about propriety.

Branek crossed his arms. "She can't know where this place is." His voice was only a hair above a whisper—just as Agnarr's had been.

"She was pretty out of it when you brought her in, so I doubt she remembers." Agnarr rubbed his beard. "We'll blindfold her down here before we leave and not take it off until we get a good distance away."

I would have to do some serious persuading to keep that from scaring her.

"Rusty Bluff—the closest town—is about ten miles west of here." Branek strode away from the wall. "I've got to check on lunch. Don't expect you all are hungry for ash."

Agnarr chuckled. "I didn't figure I'd get any better from you."

"Beggars can't be choosers." Branek stepped from the cavern.

Agnarr glanced at me, one eyebrow raised.

I merely shook my head.

He yawned. "You think she heard any of that?"

"She was sleeping really deeply when I left her." And the only part that would've disturbed her was the bit about the blindfold. If she'd been listening to their low voices.

"Keep trying to get her to tell you who her family is."

I nodded.

"How long until she can travel?"

Given that the kind of traveling she'd have to do was walk ten miles in the desert, she needed to be completely recovered. "I don't know. Everybody reacts differently to things, so I think we'll just have to see how she's doing."

And, though she'd handled her kidnapping and escape quite well so far, she could always start struggling with severe anxiety and a whole host of other problems.

Please allow her to recover with minimal effects.

He stepped up to me and tugged me into a gentle embrace. "Are you sure you didn't used to be a nurse or something?"

"I'm quite sure. I actually get rather queasy at the sight of blood. But I can make somebody comfortable and help them get rehydrated just fine."

"I'm glad." He eased back. "Tending to her would've been way above my pay grade."

"Then I'd better not get sick." I smiled at him.

He eyed me. "You're my wife. I'll make an exception for you."

"I would hope so."

He whisper-laughed, and I joined him.

Heaviness tugged at my eyelids, and I situated myself against the rock wall.

In a few minutes, I'd be joining Eldina in sleep.

She lay in peaceful stillness, a light blanket pulled to her chin.

It was a good thing Branek had found her when he did. She wouldn't have lasted many more hours out there.

I blinked hard to hold back the encroaching sleep.

"Svana." Branek's whisper came from outside the room.

I stood, and blood returned to my legs in a rush of prickles.

I stumbled from the room. "Yes?"

He tipped his head toward the main cavern, torch in hand. "Come on. Agnarr said you'd get a kick out of seeing the cave vegetables."

"Will I still be able to enjoy eating them after I see them?"

"I don't see why not."

That's what he said now.

I tucked a strand of hair behind my ear. "Do you think it's all right if I leave Eldina? She's asleep."

He nodded. "You'll be able to hear her if she needs something or yells for you."

That settled it. I needed to move around some, or I was going to fall asleep.

I followed him across the main cavern, down another tunnel, and into a cavern twice the size of the one I considered main.

Agnarr stood off to the side, hands tucked in his pockets.

Leafy carrot tops, huge potato plants, and heads of cabbage sprouted from the dirt. Every single one of them pale as could be.

"That is ... disturbing."

Branek plastered his hand to his chest. "That hurts."

"They taste good, but they're very odd." To put it lightly.

And something—some sort of cross between a spider and a cricket—hopped onto a head of cabbage.

I pointed at it while taking a step back. "What is that?"

Agnarr frowned at the thing.

Branek grinned. "A cave cricket."

"How wonderful." I took another step back. And there was another one jumping near the carrots.

This place was infested.

I folded my arms across my stomach. "So ... do the cave vegetables grow by themselves, or did you have to plant them?"

Branek got his grin under control. "There were a few of each growing when I got here, but I've cultivated them. I guess the natives who lived here before grew them."

"Eldina said natives killed the men who kidnapped her. Are these natives normally dangerous?"

Branek shook his head. "As long as you treat them with respect, they'll do the same for you. I've never had any problems with them."

Agnarr cleared his throat. "What about the tribe that lived down here?"

"I've asked the natives about that, but they don't know. Apparently, it was a different tribe." Branek shrugged. "But the ones I know aren't a fan of caves—something to do with their religion—so they don't care if I live down here."

He understood this part of the wastelands far better than I ever had. Then again. I'd mostly lived in the towns.

Branek ran his hand through his hair. "I was thinking ..."

Agnarr punched him in the shoulder. "Don't do that."

I restrained a laugh. "What were you thinking?"

Agnarr met my gaze, his grin crinkling the skin around his eyes. "Don't know if he was successful."

Branek grumbled something under his breath. "Quit it."

I cleared my throat. "You were thinking ...?"

"Yeah. That you and Eldina might like to clean up in the river. The part you saw is pretty fast moving, but a little farther down is a pool that's calm. It's cold, so you wouldn't be able to stay in long though."

To be able to wash all the dust off my skin would be glorious. Sponge baths only went so far.

Agnarr punched Branek's shoulder yet again. "You don't make much use of that pool."

"Sure I do. I visit it once a month whether I need it or not."

A complete lie. Despite his dusty clothes and unkempt hair and beard, he didn't smell. Or maybe I'd become accustomed enough to my own body odor that such a thing didn't bother me anymore.

Not a pleasant thought.

"I'll run the idea by her when she wakes up." Which was as good of a reminder as any that I'd better get back to her. "Thanks for showing me the cave vegetables."

He tipped an imaginary hat to me.

I left him and Agnarr laughing and headed back to Eldina's room.

She stirred.

I froze. Leave it to me to wake her up. Surely I hadn't been that loud. Surely she'd go back to sleep.

Or maybe it was time for her to wake up. She'd spent most of the time since Branek had found her yesterday afternoon sleeping.

The torchlight filtering from the tunnel provided enough light for me to sneak over to the spot I'd previously occupied and sit down.

"Svana?"

Of course she'd fully woken up.

"I'm sorry I woke you."

She eased into a sitting position. "It's okay. My headache's gone, and I was ready to wake up."

I rubbed my eyes. "If you're up to it, we could bathe in the river."

"There's a river down here?"

"Yes, and apparently, there's a pool that's still enough for us to swim in."

"That sounds lovely." She pushed to her feet and folded her blanket.

I stood as well. "Wait here. I'll go get directions."

Because Branek wouldn't be happy if I let Eldina see him.

I hurried into the main cavern.

Agnarr sat at the table, a book open before him. He glanced up. "He showed me where the pool is earlier. I'll get a couple of torches and take you there."

And likely wait close enough to hear us if we needed assistance.

I gathered a couple of relatively clean blankets that could serve as towels, then returned to Eldina. "Ready?"

"Yes. I feel gritty all over."

"Same." I preceded her out of her room and headed into the main cavern.

From there, we followed Agnarr down the tunnel that led into the cavern that the river flowed through and strode along the riverbank.

He stilled and fixed one torch to the wall. "Here it is."

I stepped around him.

Connected to the river—but far removed from the rapid current—was a blue pool. A rock formation in the shape of a waterfall flowed into the pool, and stalactites hung overhead.

"It's beautiful." Eldina's voice came from beside me.

"Yes."

"Holler if you need me." Agnarr strode away, the other torch in hand.

Within seconds, I'd piled my clothing on the bank with the towels and submerged myself up to my neck in the still water.

"Cold." The word left me as a gasp. "Very, very cold."

Eldina plunged in beside me and squealed.

Thank You for this, Lord. Thank You for letting me get clean.

After I'd washed off all the accumulated dirt and grime, I waded to the bank, dried off, and tugged on my clothing.

I lowered myself to a dry rock sitting a few feet from the pool, and Eldina did the same.

Maybe now was the time to ask her a few more questions. Or maybe I could just be her friend. "I've never seen anything like this." And to think it was hidden beneath the desert.

One of those strange, pale, eyeless fish darted around in the pool.

I shuddered.

At least the thing was only a few inches long in comparison to the four-foot monsters I'd seen in the river the other day.

Eldina sighed. "I feel bad keeping things from you after everything you've done for me."

Maybe it didn't matter all that much at this point. "How're you feeling? Do you think you'll be up for the hike to Rusty Bluff soon?"

"I'm feeling a lot better. Probably the day after tomorrow." She glanced at me, gaze all too studious. "I imagine you all have secrets of your own. For one, I've heard your husband's friend's voice, but I've never seen him."

This wasn't a good topic. "I suppose we all have secrets of one sort or the other."

Yet hopefully those secrets wouldn't be our downfall.

Chapter 6

The faintest hint of dawn tinged the horizon.

His canteen slapped a steady rhythm against his hip, and Svana and Eldina's quiet conversation mingled with the thud of their footsteps.

"Doing all right?"

They glanced his way, faces grayish in the dim light. Both of them wore woven hats that Branek had gotten from the natives.

"Yes." Svana smiled.

Eldina nodded.

At least she hadn't made a fuss about wearing a blindfold when they'd left the cave.

"Good. We should make Rusty Bluff well before the sun gets too hot." As long as they could keep up the current pace and didn't encounter any trouble.

That might be asking too much.

He pushed his woven hat back on his head.

The desert lay still—studded with boulders, cacti, and brush. Still was a good thing.

He brushed the gun holstered at his waist, then ran his finger across the row of cartridges secured side by side on his gun belt. "Got your pepper spray?"

She glanced his way and frowned. "Yes. Is something wrong?"

"Nope. I'm making sure you're set if something comes up."

He should've seen if Branek had a gun she could've borrowed. Even though she was more comfortable with the pepper spray, she'd said she was a decent shot with both a revolver and a rifle.

Eldina eyed him, mouth pinched.

He palmed the air. "Everything's fine." But preparation was key in case things disintegrated into something that was far from fine.

She blinked a couple of times, and her chin wobbled.

Now, he'd gone and made her feel like crying.

"Svana …"

Svana looped an arm around Eldina's shoulders and shot him a discrete smile. "Agnarr will do everything possible to keep us safe. I trust him, and even more, I trust that God is in control."

She trusted him.

Something warmed in his chest.

Eldina stepped away from Svana's partial embrace. "I'm not a particularly religious person."

He cleared desert grit from his throat. "Maybe it's time for that to change."

"Maybe." She let out a shaky laugh. "Have you ever been to Rusty Bluff?"

He shook his head. "I'm what you could call a recent exile."

"The Fairrlandian accent gives you away."

Svana chuckled. "That's what I told him. I've been to Rusty Bluff before, but I didn't stay very long. From what I can remember, it's just a dusty town with a lot of saloons."

That sounded like every other town they'd been through.

Yet they wouldn't stay in Rusty Bluff long enough for trouble to find them in the form of angry mobs or old enemies. Just long enough to ensure Eldina had a safe place to stay and a sure way of contacting her family.

Eldina curled her arms to her stomach. "I've never been there. I was born on a ranch outside of Long Gulch, moved into Long Gulch when I married, and haven't really traveled until recently."

"We'll get you settled." Yet another person who had to suffer through his poor attempts at comfort.

"Yes." Svana touched Eldina's arm. "We're not leaving until we're sure you're fine. But I know you want your privacy when you contact your family."

Eldina dipped her head. "I just ... I just don't want to get hurt."

Either she belonged to a hated family or she'd become paranoid after her kidnapping.

"You're fine." Svana rubbed the woman's shoulder. "We're not going to hurt you. I don't care who you're related to."

Eldina shrugged but lowered her arms to her sides.

He grinned at her. "Just make sure you speak highly of us to this family of yours. We don't need any more trouble."

She gave a faint laugh—but a faint laugh was better than no laugh at all. "You all have been nothing but kind to me. I'd have been dead if not for you and your friend. Who is he, by the way? I never met him."

Digging, that's what she was doing. Given her and Svana's conversation at the pool, she well knew Branek didn't care to reveal his identity to her.

"A man with about as many secrets as you."

"Fair enough." She stared off into the desert, her gaze distant.

Svana looped her arm through his. "I, for one, wish I could visit that lovely little pool every day. Especially now. I'm all dusty again."

After they got Eldina settled in town, they'd head back to Branek's then decide what to do. They couldn't continue to take advantage of Branek's hospitality even though Branek had assured him he didn't mind them staying as long as they needed.

"I know." Eldina's voice took on a wistful edge. "If I knew where that place was, I'd go back and visit it."

Then it was a good thing they'd made use of the blindfold. Branek didn't need trigger-happy gunfighters showing up on his doorstep.

"But I won't. I respect his privacy, and I'm glad you've respected mine."

Just so long as that respect didn't get them into trouble.

Step after step rattled through me, and the morning sun beamed hotter.

Yet maybe we could make it to Rusty Bluff before the sun blazed its hottest and we had to stop to seek shade.

A low-slung cliff stretched to my left. Boulders sat on my right—each with between ten and twenty yards of scruffy desert separating them.

Plenty of opportunities for shelter should we need it.

Eldina slouched along beside me.

I brushed her shoulder. "Are you doing all right? Make sure you drink enough water."

Yes, I likely sounded like her mother, but she didn't need to get dehydrated after everything she'd been through.

She uncapped her canteen and took a sip. "I'm fine."

"Make sure you keep drinking." Well, now I sounded even more like her mother. At least I was getting some practice in for any children I might have in the future.

But it'd probably be best for me to practice on someone who wasn't as close to my own age.

"How much farther do you think it is?" I aimed that question at Agnarr.

He scratched his beard. "Three or four more miles."

We could make it before we needed to stop for shade.

I licked my lips and gained a mouthful of grit. A swig from my canteen washed most of it down.

"Let's walk over by the boulders." Agnarr nudged my arm. "We'll get some shade that way."

A good idea.

I linked arms with Eldina, and we headed that way.

It was the gesture of a friend, yet it was also a not-so-obvious way of providing her with a little support.

Even though she claimed to be recovered, she'd still likely tire easily after her ordeal.

I stepped into the shadow of a boulder, and the temperature dropped several degrees.

I let out a sigh of relief.

Agnarr chuckled.

"What can I say? It feels good." Not as wonderful as that gorgeous pool in the cave but still good.

Oh, I needed to stop thinking about the icy glory of that water.

Which apparently was a little harder than it should be. Maybe I should think about that disturbing fish I'd been swimming with.

Yet fish or no fish, I'd jump into that pool in an instant if the opportunity presented itself.

Thankfully Agnarr couldn't hear my thoughts. He wouldn't think I was much of a trooper right now.

"Behind that boulder! Now!" Agnarr's voice was nothing but a bellow.

I scrambled behind the boulder, pushing Eldina ahead of me, and slammed to the ground.

The crack of gunfire reverberated through the desert.

Agnarr landed beside me, revolver in hand.

"No. No. No. No." Eldina took up the chant echoing in my head.

I wrapped a shaking arm around her. "It's okay. It's okay."

Agnarr had shouted the warning in time. He must've seen the glint of sun on a gun barrel.

He crept to the edge of the boulder and fired a return shot.

My ears rang in protest.

We couldn't have made it to Rusty Bluff without trouble.

I pulled in a ragged breath heavy with dust and the sour scent of our sweat.

"He's up on that cliff. Got us pinned down." Agnarr spoke the words as a growl. "The boulders are too far apart for us to run to the next one." He coughed. "Stay low."

Another shot blasted from the cliff, and rock sprayed off Agnarr's side of the boulder.

I wouldn't flinch. I wouldn't. "He can't see over the top of this boulder?"

"Boulder's too high, and that cliff's too low. As long as we stay close to the base, we should be fine."

Good.

"What if he changes positions?" I needed to stop asking questions. I didn't need to be distracting.

"The cliff isn't long enough for him to get much of a better angle."

Please, Lord, let us get out of this without being shot.

We should've stayed with Branek for another day.

Eldina shook against my arm.

"It's okay. Everything's going to be okay. This isn't one of your kidnappers." Yet encountering a robber after an experience like hers wasn't comforting.

Another rifle shot exploded a plume of dust to Eldina's right.

She pressed closer against me.

Agnarr returned fire.

Trembling fought for control of my muscles. But no, I had to be calm. I forced my features into neutrality and took breath after slow breath.

The shaking receded.

"Svana."

I met Agnarr's eyes.

"Put your back against the rock and watch behind us."

I did as he'd said, the boulder scraping at my shoulder blades.

Open land lay in front of me, shimmering in the heat, and boulders similar in size to the one that sheltered us lurked on either side.

At least it'd be easy for me to see anyone who would attempt a foolish attack from the rear. And even if the marauder approached from the side, he'd have a hard time doing it without me seeing since the boulders didn't form a straight line.

"It's clear." The words scraped my gritty throat. But I needed to save the water in my canteen. Who knew how long we'd be camped out here.

Yet surely the gunman would give up before dark.

Unless …

"Do you think he's part of the mob from Clear Bend?" Yet how would he have found us so conveniently?

Agnarr shook his head. "I don't know what this is."

Eldina shifted around until she too sat with her back to the boulder and drew her knees to her chest.

Please guard us, Lord. Please let that man go on his way.

My chest and throat constricted, but I breathed through it.

Another shot blasted from atop the cliff.

I fisted my hands.

This time, Agnarr didn't return fire. Likely because he didn't care to waste ammo if he didn't have a clear view of his target.

And maybe his revolver couldn't even reach that far.

"What do you want?" The boulders played back Agnarr's shout.

Another shot that sent rock chips flying was the man's reply.

Everything about this situation was nonsense.

Agnarr braced his free hand against the boulder. Heat built in his chest and rivaled the sun's rays beaming down on his shoulders and back.

If not for this interruption, they'd be close to Rusty Bluff by now. Eldina would be able to contact her family, and he and Svana would be free to return to Branek's and plan their next steps.

Either the gunman needed to get in a position that would provide a clear shot or the man needed to get out of here.

He tilted his head over his shoulder.

Svana sat motionless, dust streaking her pale face.

"Still clear?"

"Yes."

The hat and pack he'd removed minutes ago sat beside her.

He faced forward once again.

Lead scored along the boulder, skimming a trail about three feet above his head.

Either the guy was the worst of shots or he was attempting to keep them pinned down.

Yet for what reason?

No one had been following them. He'd been on guard and would've seen the signs.

Maybe this was random. A desperate exile looking to find an easy victim for his next robbery.

But it was nearly too random to be random.

Another shot blazed against the boulder.

No use firing back. That'd only waste ammo, and he didn't have an endless supply.

What he needed to do was round that cliff and sneak up behind the gunman. But that would leave Svana and Eldina unprotected. Sure, Svana had her pepper spray, but that was no match against a bullet.

"Agnarr!" Svana's voice skated about an octave higher than it normally did. "I saw movement by the boulder closest to our right."

Not good. Not good at all.

And how had someone gotten over there?

He ducked in front of them. "Get as close to the rock as you can."

Fabric scuffed rock behind him.

Sure enough, a flash of movement came from the boulder opposite theirs.

He fired.

As did the shooter on the cliff.

So there were two of them.

"Hold your fire. Both of you." Movement again flashed behind the boulder. "Let my wife come to me, and we'll all go on our way."

Eldina darted to his side.

He shot his arm out and pushed her behind him. "Is he your husband?"

"Yes."

A strange turn of events.

But it stood to reason that the shooter on the cliff was with Eldina's husband. "Tell your man to hold his fire and come down off that cliff where I can see him."

"They've helped me, Leif." Eldina pushed around him yet again. "They saved my life."

Leif. How probable was it that Eldina's husband was Leif Havard?

"Then they'll come out in the open. My man's coming down."

The rasp of falling rocks and scrambling footsteps came from the cliff.

Given that he was out of uniform and had grown a beard, he wouldn't be all that recognizable to Havard.

And at least fifteen yards would separate them.

Protect us.

He tilted his head over his shoulder.

Svana had stood, both hands knotted in front of her.

"Stay close. Get behind me, then dive for cover if there's trouble."

She gave a faint nod.

He holstered his revolver and stepped away from the boulder's shelter.

Eldina dashed toward the boulder that obscured Havard.

The man stepped clear of it, caught her in a brief embrace, then nudged her behind him.

A bearded man who must've been the shooter on the cliff shuffled to Havard's side, puffing and red-faced.

Havard glared at him. "You fool. Shooting at my wife."

The man ducked his head. "I thought she was in trouble—being that she wasn't with your men. I had to keep them in place until you came up. And I hoped you were close enough to the tunnel's mouth to hear the shots and come running."

Havard cursed. "Fool."

Tunnel. That must've been how Havard had gotten behind that boulder without Svana seeing him. The tunnel must've had an exit close by.

But at least Havard's attention wasn't on him.

"There are lots of legends of hidden treasure in tunnels in this region." Svana's voice came low beside him. "At least that's what Branek was telling me."

Havard was supposed to be gambling in Long Gulch. Not hunting for legendary treasure in the middle of a desert while his wife was kidnapped.

Havard glanced behind him. "How'd you end up traveling with these people? You were supposed to be traveling with my men. And you were supposed to arrive tomorrow."

Eldina peeked out from behind him. "We ended up leaving early. We'd stopped for the night, and two men kidnapped me. I managed to escape from them when natives attacked and killed them. Then a friend of Agnarr's found me, and Svana cared for me."

She'd had to mention his name.

Yet it was a rather common name, and Havard had only known him as Captain Vev.

"Now that she's safe with you, we'll be on our way."

Havard stared him down. "I'd like to properly thank the man who saved my wife."

He held up one hand. "No thanks needed. I'm glad she's safe and back with you."

Even though Eldina deserved a better husband than Leif Havard.

He nudged Svana's arm. "Let's get out of here."

Turning his back on Havard wouldn't be the smartest thing he'd ever done, but it was better than the alternative of hanging around any longer.

She picked up the pack and handed him his hat.

He nudged her in front of him, settled the hat on his head, and strode away from the boulder.

"Goodbye!" Eldina's lighthearted farewell carried across the desert.

Sure, it was impolite to leave without a proper goodbye, but it was also impolite to put Svana in a bad situation or bleed out on the ground.

He lifted a hand in farewell.

Svana glanced over her shoulder. "Goodbye, Eldina."

"Wait." Havard's voice came hard. "I know you."

"Keep walking." The words gritted through his teeth.

"Stop." Now that was the voice of a man with a gun in his hand.

"Leif. They're friends. They saved my life. Please put that away."

Eldina's plea added credence to his suspicions.

He gave the pack on Svana's back a gentle shove. "Keep walking. You know the way back to Branek's."

Then he turned to face Havard. "Put the gun away. There's no need for it."

Eldina tugged on Havard's gun arm. "Please, Leif."

Please don't let me have to shoot Havard in front of his wife. Please don't let me have to shoot him at all.

Havard scowled at him, gun held in a hand all too steady. "I know you."

He'd confront the man's suspicions head on. "Yeah, you do. I stopped you from assassinating one of the king's advisors."

Havard gave a short nod. "Vev. I should kill you."

"No." Eldina tugged on his arm. "Please don't. They saved my life."

Havard didn't spare her so much as a glance.

This was nonsense. Complete nonsense. "We're both exiles now. There's no score to settle."

"Listen to him, Leif." Eldina jerked his arm. "Please, please listen to him. They're good people. They took care of me when they had no reason to. They were taking me to Rusty Bluff so I could contact you."

Havard shook her off, his features hard. "Here's the deal, Vev. Just this once, I'll let you go. But if we ever come face to face again, nothing is going to stop me from putting a bullet in you."

There'd be no reason for him to run across Havard again. Unless the man continued popping out of random holes in the ground.

He gave Havard a nod, then turned and walked toward Svana.

I'd almost lost him.

I sat in the single chair in the coolness of Branek's main cavern.

Agnarr's and Branek's voices echoed from another part of the cave, rising and falling as Agnarr told what'd happened.

I'd almost lost him.

And if he ever ran across Havard again, I could very well lose him.

Because unlike the mercy God had shown me, Havard's mercy had to be earned by the recipient.

The voices cut off, then Agnarr strode into the main cavern.

I slipped into his embrace and just held on.

He rubbed a slow circle on my back. "Branek told me there's a rancher about fifteen miles from here who employs some of Branek's native friends. These natives told Branek the man's looking to hire some guards. Apparently, he's got a lot of enemies. Word is he's hired several former members of the royal guard and doesn't care as long as they're good workers."

I eased back just a step. "What if others find out you're working there and assume you're a royal guard?"

"It's already happened once. We'll just have to play it by ear. But from what Branek's friends say, nobody wants to mess with this rancher. He's got a reputation for being tough and no-nonsense."

Maybe this would work. Maybe we'd at least get to stay there for more than a couple of days. "This rancher wouldn't have a problem with me being with you?"

He shook his head. "He's also looking for some women to help his wife out around the house."

Well, I could do that.

He met my eyes. "I've been praying—asking God for wisdom—and I think we should see how this turns out."

I nodded. "It sounds just fine to me."

And it was fifteen miles farther from Havard. "Will he try to track you down?"

He rubbed the back of his neck. "I don't know the future, but he seemed to have his mind more on lost treasure or whatever he was doing down in that tunnel than on killing me. In the grand scheme of things, I'm not that important to him."

I could hope.

A shudder rippled across my skin.

No. Whatever happened, my hope was in God.

I willed a smile to my lips. "When do we leave?"

He grinned back at me. "Tomorrow."

Author's Note

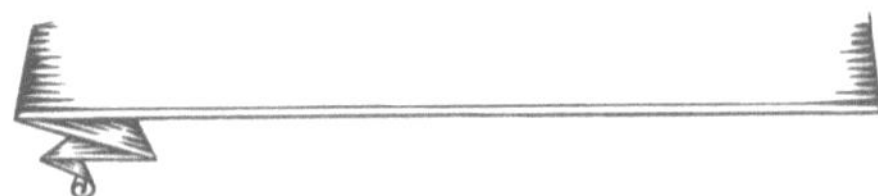

I hope you enjoyed this first installment of The Rykfallinn Chronicles. Thanks so much for reading it!

As for what's next ... I've got some exciting projects in the works. I'm drafting the sequel to *Trouble in Dry Springs*. I also have a novella that is due to be featured in an upcoming fantasy anthology, and I'm working on ideas for the second installment in The Rykfallinn Chronicles. Follow me on Instagram to keep track of any updates: https://www.instagram.com/kristinahallwriter/

And finally, if you're someone who likes reviewing books, I'd love it if you'd leave an honest review of *Exiled* on the site(s) of your choice. Reviews are a great way for other readers to find new books.

For His glory,
Kristina Hall

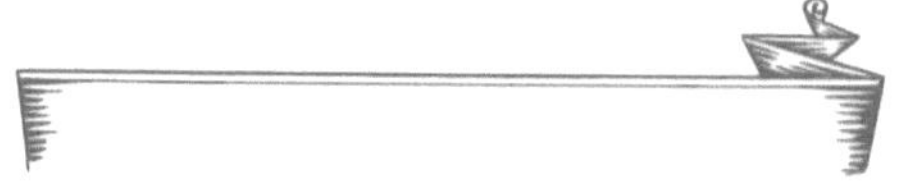

Acknowledgments

My Lord and Savior, Jesus Christ—Thank You for getting me through another book!

Dad—Thanks for always supporting my writing!

Mom—Thank you for extracting all my silly mistakes! You're the best editor ever!

Vanessa—Thanks for reading everything I write!

And for the images on the cover—© Ирина Харченко / Depositphotos.com, © Brent Coulter / Depositphotos.com, and © Maxim Chuev / Depositphotos.com. Thanks!

Don't miss out!

Visit the website below and you can sign up to receive emails whenever Kristina Hall publishes a new book. There's no charge and no obligation.

https://books2read.com/r/B-A-BCBN-GKXLC

Connecting independent readers to independent writers.

Did you love *Exiled*? Then you should read *Trouble in Dry Springs*[1] by Kristina Hall!

[2]

Even the peaceful town of Dry Springs is not without trouble. When Eliza McCoslin's brother sends for her, she exchanges war-torn Mississippi for Dry Springs, Texas. Settling into a new way of life proves difficult though, despite the arrival of the man she's long admired.Jesse Carrigan comes to Dry Springs seeking work and a place to start the ranch he's dreamed of ever since his parents lost their farm. What he doesn't expect to find is the woman he'd like to court—or his former colonel on the run from a deadly threat.Given the

---

1. https://books2read.com/u/4Ngo9N

2. https://books2read.com/u/4Ngo9N

circumstances keeping Jesse and Eliza apart and the danger looming on the horizon, he and Eliza find themselves facing the loss of future love—and life. When trouble comes to Dry Springs, who will be left standing?

Read more at https://kristinahallauthor.wordpress.com/.

Also by Kristina Hall

A Better Country
Strangers and Pilgrims
To the Uttermost

Kentucky Midnight
Midnight Will Come
Darkness Draws Near
Shadows Close In

Refuge
Fled for Refuge
Refuge from the Storm
Place of Refuge

Science Falsely So Called
Things Not Seen

Stand

The Dry Springs Chronicles
Trouble in Dry Springs

The Moretti Trilogy
Promises Unbroken
Mercy Undeserved
Truth Unshaken

The Rykfallinn Chronicles
Exiled

Watch for more at https://kristinahallauthor.wordpress.com/.

About the Author

Kristina Hall is a sinner saved by grace who seeks to glorify God with her words. She is a homeschool graduate and holds a degree in accounting. When she's not writing, she enjoys reading, arm wrestling, lifting weights, and playing the violin.

Read more at https://kristinahallauthor.wordpress.com/.

9 798223 354154